Gay on a TRAIN

K.C. WELLS

This is a work of fiction. Names, characters, places, and incidents either are the product of the author's imagination or are used fictitiously, and any resemblance to actual persons, living or dead, business establishments, events, or locales is entirely coincidental.

Cover content is being used for illustrative purposes only and any person depicted on the cover is a model.

The trademarked products mentioned in this book are the property of their respective owners and are recognized as such.

#loveWins

love is love

This book came about because of a post from Reddit back in 2016.

I have no idea if the straight guy went on his date with the gay man on the train who asked him out.

I hope he did.

The romantic soul in me hopes it was magical, and that they're still together today.

This is *my* version of 'what happened next'…

Chapter 1

June 8, 2018

You know how some people have premonitions? Maybe they wake up one morning and they just *know* something's going to happen? They feel it in their water?

Well, before you get all excited, I'm not one of those people. Sorry. And that particular day—I've come to think of it as *The Day*—was nothing out of the ordinary. I woke up late—which I do way too often—so that meant I was dashing about like a blue-arsed fly, trying to get to work on time and *not* look like I'd been dragged through a hedge backward. Work was boring as fuck—no change there—and I kept watching the clock because when the day was done, my weekend would *finally* start. Not that my weekends were all *that* riveting. I mean, we're talking laundry, shopping, tidying my room…

Yeah, I know. Excitement, right? But it was better than being at work, answering customers' BMW calls—that's Bitching, Moaning & Whining to those of you not in the know. How I manage to sound calm when offering such advice as 'Well, have you tried switching it off, then switching it back on again?' I'll never know. Because sometimes… just sometimes… it's right on the tip of my tongue to say, 'Well, if you had more than two brain cells to rub together, you'd have read the instruction manual before calling me. Have a nice day.'

Yeah, no. That would be my P45 handed to me before you could say 'Hello, Jobseeker's Allowance.'

But anyway, back to that day…

I really hate traveling to work right now. Bloody trains. It wasn't always this bad. I could get from Reading into London in under half an hour, until they introduced a one-way system at London Paddington, and now some journeys can take up to an hour. Add to that a supervisor who makes sure I don't leave before I've given them their pound of flesh, and that means if I make it onto the 18.04, I'm doing really well. Any later, and it's gone seven o'clock by the time I'm walking through my front door.

See what I mean? My life is just one big quivering heap of excitement, right? And I keep wandering off the point of this, which is *that day*…

I was waiting at Paddington for the 18.04—yeah, it was a good day—and I was on my phone as usual, scrolling through Facebook and Instagram. Cheryl popped up in my feed, and of course I had to click on her post. It was five months since we broke up, after a year together. From the look of things, she had a new fella. I was glad. It hadn't been a nasty breakup—we just wanted different things: she wanted a wedding ring, and I didn't. Like I said, no nastiness, just a mutual decision to end it. Since Cheryl, I'd been out on maybe ten or so dates, and two or three of them had ended up with us having sex. So I wasn't exactly a hermit. I was happy to keep things casual. Not to mention, I was only just getting used to life as a single guy again.

Anyway, back to Paddington…

I was sitting on one of those hard-as-fuck stainless steel benches. You know the ones, designed to make your arse go numb after sitting on one for more than thirty seconds. (They don't *want* you sitting, okay? Makes the place look untidy.) The train was due to pull out in about five minutes, which of course meant it hadn't even arrived yet from its previous journey. What was that slogan again about the trains? 'Wonderfully predictable'? Well, I don't know about the wonderfully part, but as for the rest, unfortunately yes.

Anyway, this guy sat on the seat next to mine, and he looked pissed off.

Now, I'll talk to anyone, okay? And someone looking as pissed off as *he* did was crying out to be talked to.

"Bad day?" I gave him a sympathetic glance.

He rolled his eyes. "They cancelled my train. That means I won't get into Newbury now till 6.45."

I huffed. "Tell me about it. If my supervisor—she with a face like a slapped arse and about as much personality as my drier's lint filter—had had *her* way, I'd still be at my desk." Just because she caught me talking about her, the cow.

(Well, she *is* a cow! Ask anyone.)

He snorted. "Okay, *that* paints a picture." He glanced up at the train info and sighed. "Great. 'Expected at 18.08'."

"Look on the bright side," I suggested. "At least it's running." That was my train too.

He pulled his phone from his bag and scowled. "This is *not* my day. Battery's dying."

I had to do something to cheer him up. I peered at his phone, then pulled out my power bank and USB cord from my bag. It's a hefty little thing, but it can do a load of recharges before it needs topping up. "Here." I held them out to him.

He stared at it like he'd never seen one.

"We're on the same train," I explained. "I get off the stop before you. That gives you about nineteen minutes by my reckoning to put some juice into yours."

And just like that, his expression melted into this great smile. "Really? Aw, that's good of you." It was the kind of smile you'd notice.

"Just don't forget to find me before we

reach Reading," I told him. Yeah, I know I should have been worried that he might disappear on me, but you know what? I knew he wouldn't. Just a feeling. Maybe it was that smile.

Right then, a computer-generated voice told us the train was arriving, so we headed for the ticket barrier. We waited there while the train disgorged its passengers onto the platform, who then trudged toward us, tickets or Oyster cards in their hands. Once they were through, it was our turn, a mass of commuters all trying to get through the barriers without them telling us to 'seek assistance.'

(Isn't technology wonderful? Yeah—wonderfully predictable. Or should that be 'woefully'?)

I walked as far as I could down the platform, like I always did. My gran used to say, 'Observe the masses and do the opposite.' So I let my fellow commuters dive onto the first coach they found. Not me, thank you very much. I had no desire to be a sardine for nineteen minutes.

(I know what you're thinking. How sad it is that I know exactly how long my train journey would be? Well, trust me, if you relied on the rail network to get *you* to work on time, you'd know too.)

(And I am *not* sad, okay?)

Then I remembered. It might have been a good idea to let what's-his-face know where I was going, yeah? So he could return my power bank?

(I swear, sometimes my brain goes out and doesn't tell me what time it's coming back.)

"Wait up!" What's-his-face was sprinting along the platform toward me.

I paused at the door to the front coach and smiled at him. "I'm glad one of us has some sense."

He laughed. "God, you move fast." He waited for me to get onto the train, then followed me into the coach. I headed for the seats in the middle, the only ones with a table. I slid into a front-facing window seat. What's-his-face paused in the aisle beside me.

"Is it okay if I take this seat?" He gestured to the one facing mine.

"Sure." It was no skin off my nose. It made sense, actually.

He sat, keeping his bag on his lap. A minute later, the train lurched forward, and began its slow pull out of the station. I leaned back in my seat, my phone still in my hand, while he attached his to the power bank. I took a moment to study him as surreptitiously as I could.

I'd have to say one word summed him up—pretty. He was possibly my age, with dark brown eyes, and long, black lashes that curved on his cheeks as he gazed at his phone. His suspiciously creamy, flawless cheeks… *Is he wearing make-up?* That glint on his lips had to be a gloss of some kind. Of course, it could have been lip balm for all I knew. *That bone structure...* I knew several women who would kill to have his cheekbones. His hair was perfectly coiffed, liked he'd just stepped out of a salon. Dark brown hair, short at the sides, longer on top where it was highlighted. His hands were slim, with long fingers ending in beautifully manicured nails.

Maybe he's a model? His clothes were definitely stylish, from his button-down Oxford shirt in white with its pale grey stripes, to his pastel pink jacket that complimented it perfectly. His jeans should have looked all wrong with that combo, but the slim fit and washed-out look accentuated the overall effect.

I noticed the pin on the strap of his bag. The little enamel rainbow Pride pin. Then I saw there were *several* pins: a rainbow heart, a smiley badge with a rainbow background, and two pins bearing the words Love is Love, and Love Wins.

And now that I thought about it, his voice didn't make him sound like someone who could saw through tree trunks with his bare hands. Not with *those* nails, anyway.

Okay, I *might* have been wrong, but something told me What's-his-face was gay.

That didn't bother me, to be honest. I've worked with too many guys who'd run screaming from the room if they thought a gay man had so much as *breathed* on them. (What *is* it with some straight guys that they automatically assume every gay guy is trying to get into their pants?)

(In case you haven't worked it out yet? I don't much like some of the people I work with, mostly because they're complete and utter arseholes.)

"How can you have signal? I haven't even got a single bar."

I glanced across at him. "The Wi-Fi is always crap on the train. Signal keeps going in and out. I'm reading something I downloaded earlier."

He smiled. "Smart guy." He leaned back too, visibly more relaxed. "Thank you. It's been a bloody awful day, and you helping made it a bit better."

"You're welcome. And I know all about shit days, believe me."

He chuckled. "Of course you do. You work with someone who has the personality of a lint filter." He shook his head. "That was funny. Is she really that bad?"

I groaned. "Oh, God, she's *worse*. I swear, she thinks her sole purpose in that place is to bug the hell out of me." I gave him some for-instances, he started laughing, and pretty soon I was laughing too. Then he told me about some of the people he worked with, and I had to admit, one of them sounded about as emotionally deep as a puddle. It was a great conversation, and I relaxed for the first time all day.

I gave a mental nod to my more homophobic colleagues. *See? Not* all *gay men want to flirt and try it on.* Some *gay guys can just have a good chat.*

He cleared his throat. "Can I ask… what's your name? We've been talking away, and it feels weird not having a clue who I'm talking to."

"I'm Lee." He was right, of course. I couldn't keep thinking of him as what's-his-face.

He smiled. "Hello, Lee, I'm Daniel." He held out his hand, and I shook it. Except… he held onto it just a fraction longer than I'd anticipated, and his gaze met mine.

The first thought that flitted through my mind was that his eyes really were pretty. The second was that I'd never noticed a guy's eyes before.

The third was that my *God*, he was *studying* me.

Then he let go, and the moment passed.

I coughed. "So, where do you work?" I acted like nothing had happened. Except…nothing *had* happened—so why the hell did it feel like the opposite?

"I work in a male fashion shop."

"Well, that explains it," I announced.

He arched his beautiful neat brows. "Explains what?"

Shit. "Why you look the way you do. You must be a walking advert for the shop." And why the fuck did I say that? *Lee Paul Tennant, did you just flirt with that man?*

Christ, the voice in my head sounded just like Gran.

His lips twitched. "Why, thank you. That sounds like a compliment."

Okay, *that* was flirtatious. And I was getting flustered.

There were any number of things I wanted to say to him right then but didn't dare.

Are you flirting with me?

Do you think I'm gay?

I'm not going mad, am I? You are *flirting with me, aren't you?*

I could have blurted out the whole 'I'm-straight' bit, but you know what? That would only accomplish two things. It would bring an end to the great conversation, and it would make me look like an arrogant bastard who assumed Daniel wanted to get into my pants.

God, the irony.

I did my best to continue talking, but it was as if I was aware of him in a way I hadn't been before. I found myself leaning forward and smiling while we chatted. I made lots of eye contact. I raised my chin up when I spoke, because I knew it made my neck look longer.

Oh my God. What the hell am I doing?

Except I knew exactly what I was doing. The same thing I did when I was with someone I was trying to impress the hell out of. I was being subtle about it, sure, but it was like everything I did drew his attention.

Daniel kept right on studying me, like he was trying to make up his mind about something. I shoved my phone into my bag, then sat it on the table in front of me, restlessly picking at the leather label.

His gaze flickered down to my hands, then back up. "Are you nervous?"

"No," I replied instantly. I gazed at him. "What have I got to be nervous about?"

Okay, that came out as coy, and I didn't have a coy bone in my body.

Daniel laughed. "You know what, Lee? You're really cute. So… what are you doing tomorrow night?"

Wait. I'm cute?

A guy just told me I was cute.

Then the rest hit home. "Why… why do you want to know?"

He's not going to ask me out. He's not. We just met. And I'm straight, *remember?*

"Because I'd like to take you out on a date." Those deep brown eyes were focused on me. Everything about Daniel said he was being totally serious.

Okay. This was when I lost my grip on reality.

It didn't matter that he wasn't a woman. He

was an attractive, interesting man, with a good sense of humour, and a great line in conversation. My heart was racing, and my tongue slipped into autopilot before my brain had a chance to tell it to shut the fuck up.

"Sure."

What?

Chapter 2

Daniel beamed. "Great!"

What the fuck did I just do?

And before I had time to answer that question, Daniel handed over his phone, still attached to my power bank, and asked me to add my number. I did it, my head in a spin.

Why didn't I say 'Well, that's really flattering, but I'm straight'?

Why didn't I say, 'Sorry, I only date women'?

And why was my heart pounding like it was going to burst?

I knew part of the reason was the fact he looked so happy that I'd said yes. How could I say no, and crush the feelings of someone who obviously *really* liked the idea of going on a date with me?

I handed back his phone, and he glanced at it. "Lee Tennant. Any relation to David? The *sexiest* Doctor Who ever?" I think my snort was answer enough. He clicked on my number, and my phone burst into life to the tune of Addicted by Serge Devant. Daniel's face lit up in that great smile again. "I love that."

I hurriedly killed it before saving his number.

"And I'm Daniel Bond." He grinned. "Licensed to thrill." He chuckled. "Sorry. I usually slip that in before someone else makes a joke of it."

My usual quick barbs had deserted me. I was so flustered, I didn't know what to say to him.

(Oh, there were plenty of things I *could* have said—I just didn't want to say any of them, because I didn't want to hurt his feelings.)

"Text me tonight, so we can sort out what we're doing?" That smile hadn't dimmed. "You can call me too if you want. I'll be home all evening. At least you know what time I'll be pulling into Newbury."

It took me a second to remember. "6.43. Not allowing for delays."

Daniel's eyes sparkled. "That's right." He glanced through the window, then quickly detached his phone. "We're almost at Reading." He handed me the power bank and cord. When I said nothing, but stuffed them into my bag, Daniel gave me an inquiring glance. "Are you okay? This is the first time you've been quiet since I sat next to you at the station." He looked like the thought amused him.

What the hell could I say to that? *Well, actually, I'm trying to work out how to tell you that my brain just farted and what came out is 'yes, I'll go on a date with you.'*?

Then he completely derailed me. "I can't

wait for Saturday night." He said it so earnestly and with such sincerity that I didn't have the heart to disappoint him.

Then don't. Text him tonight. It'll be easier that way. You'll never have to see him again.

That calmed me down a bit, and I breathed a little easier. I must have appeared more relaxed because Daniel relaxed too.

Would it be so *bad? We could go to a club, go dancing…* I already knew his taste in music, so that wasn't too far out a suggestion. Then I checked myself. *Why am I even considering this?*

The train started slowing as it neared Reading, so I got to my feet, trying to steady myself by hanging onto the back of the seat. I grabbed my bag from the table, pasted on a hopefully bright smile, and said "See you!" Then I headed for the door to wait for the train to stop. When it did, I dive-bombed off that train and legged it to the nearest exit.

(I know what you're thinking, okay? Why was I leading Daniel on like that? And you know what? Right then, I couldn't explain it. That part came later.)

I weaved my way through Reading Station on autopilot, my mind still on Daniel's shock invitation. The house was only about five minutes from the station, and I was mentally figuring out who'd be home when I got there. Moz would still be at work at the Broad Street Mall, where he was a sales assistant in a jewellers. Mick would be home soon from the Royal Berkshire Hospital where he was IT manager. That was if he wasn't working from home, as he sometimes did. Justin would be at the local gym, training one of his clients. That left Niall, who'd probably be asleep. He worked in a bakery, and his day started very early.

By the time I reached the front door, I'd calmed down a lot. The house was quiet, and I was grateful for that. I needed a bit of peace to think things through. I walked into the kitchen at the rear of the house, smiling at the gleaming, decluttered work surfaces. That would have been Niall's doing. He always cleared away the dishes from breakfast when he got home after work. Niall was easily the most house proud of all of us housemates.

(Yeah, I know it sounds like utter pandemonium, five guys sharing a house, but it works for us. The location is brilliant for Justin, Moz, and Niall, and I'm a stone's throw from the station. We all get along—well, *most* of the time. There *has* been the occasional battle over the TV remote, but then again, there are two communal lounges, which cuts down on the disagreements.)

I filled the kettle, then grabbed the coffee jar from the cabinet and a teaspoon from the drawer. I kept replaying the conversation with Daniel over and over. We'd talked for maybe twenty minutes by the time he asked me out.

Oh my God. There was a voice in my head

yelling 'He asked me out!' You know, just in case I'd missed that part.

"Er, Lee?"

I looked toward the door where Niall stood, staring at me in obvious amusement. I arched my eyebrows. "Something funny?"

He smirked. "Yeah—your face when you try that coffee. I think you've put about six spoonfuls in that mug."

I blinked and peered into it. "Shit." I emptied it back into the jar and started again. The kettle beeped. "You want one?"

Niall nodded, stepping into the room and heading for the fridge. "I take one spoonful in my coffee, in case you were wondering."

"Sarky bastard." I grabbed him a mug and made the coffee. When I was done, he took his and went to the table at the far end, which was surrounded by five high stools. I joined him, my mind still focused on Daniel.

This is turning out to be one weird day.

Niall cleared his throat. "So… how was work?"

I stared at him. "Since when do you ask me about that? Unless you really *want* me to bore you to death."

He shrugged. "I thought it would be the quickest way to find out what's on your mind."

"And what makes you think there's anything on my mind?" I retorted.

His lips twitched. "Oh, come *on*. The coffee was a bit of a bloody giveaway."

I wasn't sure I wanted *anyone* knowing. Then I reasoned talking it through might actually help. And at least it was *Niall*. It could have been much worse. I could imagine Justin laughing his arse off.

I started with Daniel sitting next to me at the station, and ended with me getting off the train, with the promise to text or call later. Niall said nothing while I talked, just sipped his coffee. He was still quiet after I'd finished.

Finally, I gave in. "Well? Why aren't you laughing?"

Niall gave me a puzzled glance. "Oh, I'm sorry. Was it supposed to be a joke?"

Okay, my jaw might have dropped at that point. "Did you miss the part where he asked me out on a date?"

"I heard it. And?"

I glared at him. "What do you mean, 'And'?"

"Well, are you gonna go out with him?"

"Why the hell would I go on a date with a guy? I'm straight, remember?"

Niall gave me a knowing smile. "Then why did you say yes?"

"I—" I tried to regroup my thoughts. "I didn't want to hurt him." Niall chuckled, and I stared at him in surprise. "Why is that funny?"

"Oh, it's not. What tickled me is the idea of you not wanting to hurt the feelings of a guy you don't even know." His eyes gleamed. "Since when do *you* pull punches?"

(Okay. This is where I have to admit that of all the housemates, I'm the mouthy one. And Niall was right. I speak first and think later. There's a reason my mum always tells me to put my brain into gear before I put my mouth into action.)

"Is he good looking?" Niall asked suddenly.

"Yeah. He's kind of… pretty, actually." (Well, he was! I wasn't going to lie.)

He quirked his eyebrows at that but didn't comment. "And you've *never* thought about being with another guy?"

I shook my head slowly. Except…. Nope. Nope. Besides, that didn't count. All I did was *wonder* about it. And wondering wasn't the same as thinking, right?

(Yeah. I think I had a huge case of hair-splitting going on right then.)

"Ever watched gay porn?"

Okay, *that* one took me by surprise. "Strictly heterosexual." I coughed. "And… sometimes lesbian porn." Except with het porn my focus wasn't always on the girls, but I wasn't about to share *that* part.

"So watching two girls have sex is okay, but watching two blokes isn't?" There was that look of amusement again.

I snorted. "Have *you* ever watched it?"

Another shrug. "Sure. I don't have a problem with it. Some of it's hot as fuck."

There went my jaw again.

Niall laughed. "I wish you could see your face." He leaned forward, his elbows on the table, his chin resting on his laced fingers. "Daniel is obviously interested in you."

I couldn't argue with that. After all, he'd asked me out.

"Now, don't jump down my throat, okay?" Niall met my gaze. "There has to be a reason why you said yes so quickly. So forget about being straight and only dating women for a moment, and think about it. Did you feel a connection with him?"

I opened my mouth to say no, but snapped it shut. There had been something, hadn't there? That… spark when we shook hands. The way I felt when he looked me in the eye.

I swallowed. "Maybe," I said cautiously.

Niall nodded like I hadn't just surprised the hell out of him. "I think part of you is excited by the idea of going on a date with Daniel. *I* think you're more open to this than you're letting yourself believe."

"But why now?" That was the part I didn't get. "You don't suddenly start having gay thoughts at twenty-six when you haven't had them before."

"Why not?" Niall asked with a frown. "And

strictly speaking, they're not gay thoughts." He grinned. "More like bi thoughts." Then he cocked his head to one side. "Be honest. Does the idea excite you?"

I put down my mug and stared at the table, trying to put my thoughts into some semblance of order.

Does the thought repulse me? Clearly not. If it had, I wouldn't have given a flying fuck about hurting Daniel's feelings—I'd have come out with an instantaneous no.

Would I be open to something that new? Why the hell not? It wasn't *wrong*, was it?

Do I want to see where this leads? Okay, that was the slightly scary part, because one of the places it *could* lead was to a bed, and I didn't know how I felt about that. *What if he wants to sleep with me Saturday night?*

Okay, I couldn't think about that. Except… maybe mentioning to Daniel my lack of experience in the gay sex department might be something to consider.

And there it was, that slow unfurling of something in my belly. The same sensation I'd had when Daniel had given me *that look.*

(Yeah, okay, I can admit it now. It was a really flirtatious look, and no woman had *ever* looked at me like that, or made me feel so… *wanted*, and maybe *that* was why I said yes in the first place.)

I shivered. "Yes," I whispered. "It excites me."

Niall gave me a warm smile, and in my heart, I knew it was because I'd given the right answer.

"Then call him tonight, and set up a date," he said simply. Whatever else he was going to say was lost when the front door opened, and Justin entered, yelling that it was Friday night and there'd better be beer and pizza on the menu.

Niall glanced at me. "If you want to talk about this some more, you know where I am," he said quietly. "Just… no late night angsty chats, please? *Some* of us have to be up with the birds."

I laughed. "I promise." Then the door to the nearest communal lounge opened, and Mick stepped out of it, holding his laptop.

"I thought I heard voices." He grinned. "Well, I heard Justin."

As long as that was *all* he'd heard. I'd thought Niall and I were alone.

Justin marched into the kitchen and looked around. "Where are the beers? Come on, lads. I've worked off a lot of calories today. I deserve a beer or four." He grabbed the takeaway pizza menu from its home on the notice board and began perusing its contents.

"I'll go and get out of my work clothes," I muttered, stepping past Justin and heading for the stairs. My room was on the second floor.

"You've got about forty minutes before the food gets here," Justin told me. "And Moz'll be here in about ten. He's already texted me his order." He chuckled. "I already know what *you* want," he said to me. "Mr. Predictable."

It was on the tip of my tongue to say, 'Well, that's all *you* know,' but I kept my mouth shut. The fewer people who knew about this, the better.

Forty minutes before the pizza arrived. Was I going to wait until after dinner to call Daniel?

Was I fuck.

Chapter 3

I went into my room and closed the door. Despite Niall's apparent confidence that I was doing the right thing, my heart was racing. I debated texting Daniel but dismissed it.

I needed to hear his voice again.

I sat on the bed, my phone in my hand, mentally going over what I was going to say.

Okay, Daniel? There's something you should know...

Yeah, I'd love to go on a date with you. Will I need condoms?

Are we going to a gay club?

Fuck it. At this rate I'd be here until midnight.

Just make the bloody call.

I scrolled through contacts to Daniel's number, and clicked Call. He answered after only two rings. "You're eager." Even over the phone I could tell he was smiling.

(See? *This* is why voice calls beat texts any day.)

"Look, about this date…" Now that I was speaking to him, my stomach was in knots.

"You *were* nervous, weren't you?"

And the rest. Which kind of put me in a dilemma. *Do I tell him I'm not gay?* Because if I did, he might cancel the date, and I was shocked to realize I didn't want that. I wanted to see where this was going. Okay, there'd only been a brief connection, but I was intrigued and excited by it.

"It's been awhile since I dated." Well, that much was true. My last date had to have been about a month ago.

"That's okay." He chuckled. "I'm sure it will all come back to you. Anyway, I've been thinking about what we might do."

My heart went into overdrive. "Oh?"

"To be honest, it's been a busy week. Would it be okay with you if we just met up at one of our places and watched a DVD?"

Oh, I liked the sound of that. "Sure. Only I suppose this is the point where I ask what kind of films you like." I was already mentally going over a list of films he was going to come out with. *The Sound of Music*, *Priscilla, Queen of the Desert*, *The Birdcage*…

"Do you like animation?"

Yeah. Totally not what I expected, and it served me right for being so bloody presumptuous. "Yeah. I've been known to watch a few." I glanced over at the shelf in the corner of the room where my DVDs were piled. *Toy Story*, *Finding Nemo*, *The Lion King*, *Frozen*… *Dumbo*…

(You're judging me. I can feel it.)

"Have you seen *How To Train Your Dragon*?"

"I think I missed that one. Is it good?"

"It's brilliant. There have been a few sequels and they're all good. I've got the first two, and I was thinking we might manage them in one evening."

A date watching animated films. I could go with that. "That sounds great. Er… where? I'd say here, but trust me, you wouldn't want that." And I *definitely* didn't. My housemates would have a field day.

"Okay, now I'm intrigued."

"I share a house with four other blokes. Most evenings here are like organized chaos." And besides, how the hell would I explain Daniel?

"Well, how about my place then? You okay with coming to Newbury?"

I had no problem with that. It was only about twenty minutes on the train from Reading. "Yeah, that's fine. Just text me your address."

"It's just me, by the way. I live in a two-bedroom flat close to the station." He paused. "Look… do you want to eat before we watch the films? I can cook. Well… sort of. I *am* trying to improve my culinary skills. Failing that, there's a fab Italian restaurant around the corner that does takeaway." He chuckled. "That might be a safer bet, now that I think about it."

"Works for me." I loved Italian. Okay… I

don't know what came over me. We'd been talking calmly, and he seemed okay with me not having dated recently. So I have no idea why my mouth ran away with me. "You were right. I *am* nervous. It's just…" I took a deep breath. "I haven't ever been out with a guy before."

There was a moment of silence, and I felt sure I blown it. "It's okay, really." His voice was gentle, and just the sound of it eased my racing heartbeat. "Like I said on the train, you're cute, and I'd really like to see you again." Another pause. "If you want to change your mind, that's okay too."

But I *didn't* want to change my mind.

"I want to see you again too." And that was the absolute truth.

"Great." I could hear the relief in his voice. "How does seven o'clock sound?"

"Sounds good. I'll be there. Do you want me to bring anything?"

Daniel chuckled. "Just you, cutie." And then he disconnected.

My heart was hammering. *I did it. I'm going on a date—with a guy.* And I didn't have a fucking clue what to expect. *Cutie?*

I took a look in the mirror. *What does he see that I don't?* My hair kind of… flopped, my chin was huge, my jawline was too square, I had lips like a girl….

Fuck. *It was my lips, wasn't it? He was looking at my lips and thinking of kissing them.*

Only, that got *me* thinking about kissing *him*, imagining how it would feel. His face was smooth, so no beard rash to consider. And his lips looked like they'd be soft.

That was it, I'd lost it. I was standing in front of my mirror, my mind full of Daniel kissing me, and the idea was… pleasant. Exciting.

Okay—it was also arousing. (Happy now? So what if the thought of Daniel kissing me was turning me on? Hmm? If I'm open to dating a guy, why can't I be open to… other things?)

Even if those other things sent shivers through me.

"Lee! Pizza!"

I blinked, then looked at my bedside alarm clock. *No fucking way*. I'd only been on the phone for a couple of minutes. Then I realized I'd spent most of the time wondering what the fuck I was going to say to him. (And the time spent fantasizing about him kissing me. Yeah, I didn't forget that part.)

"Coming." I shucked off my suit and shirt, and squirmed into my jeans. By the time I got to the kitchen, the rest of them were gathered around, opening pizza boxes, dividing up garlic bread and wedges, and dishing out coleslaw.

Justin grinned when he saw me. "Yours is the Hawaiian, right?" He gave an exaggerated shudder. "Pineapple on a pizza."

Mick elbowed him. "I noticed you wolfed

down all those cheese/pineapple/cocktail sausages on stick things we had for Moz's birthday party." His eyes glittered.

Justin blinked. "Yeah, well, I was being polite."

Mick snorted. "*Polite* would've been to eat one or two. If I recall, you ate most of them."

I just stood back and enjoyed the floorshow.

Justin gaped at him. "But… this is *pizza*." He said it like it explained everything. "It's just… weird."

Moz snickered. "Says you, who likes anchovies on his pizza." He mimicked Justin's shudder perfectly, and the others laughed.

Niall poured Coke into a glass. "Anyone else not on the beer?" He rolled his eyes. "And I wasn't asking *you*," he flung at Justin. That got another laugh.

When they all had food, we went into the nearest lounge, and Niall switched on the TV. Mick quickly grabbed the remote. "Nope. We are *not* watching the One Show," he said emphatically, but with a twinkle in his eyes. "You want to do that, go elsewhere."

"Is anyone going out tonight?" Justin asked between bites.

Moz shook his head. "I'm knackered."

"How can you be knackered?" Justin exclaimed. "All you do is stand behind a counter all day looking bored out of your skull." He grinned. "Oh, apart from those times where someone wants to see a pair of ten quid earrings from the window."

Moz spluttered Coke all over his pizza. "Ten quid? I can see it's been a while since *you* bought earrings for a girlfriend."

"Yeah, well, usually it's the girls who buy stuff for me." Justin preened.

"Do they think the only way they'll get you to stay away is to bribe you? Is that it?" Mick asked innocently.

"At least I go out on dates," Justin retorted good-naturedly. "The only thing *you* gaze at with longing is the latest gadget."

"So what?" Niall chuckled. "There are gadgets now for all kinds of… needs." His lips twitched. "Maybe Mick's got the right idea. You don't have to take a *gadget* out for dinner or to a club. Gadgets don't want presents. Just keep 'em juiced up and… cleaned."

(Okay, you do *not* want to know where my mind went.)

It seemed Mick's sense of humour was on a similar wavelength to Niall's. "Yeah, some are even waterproof." He waggled his eyebrows.

It was my turn to splutter Coke.

Justin gazed at me, Mick and Niall. "You think you know people, and suddenly…" When Mick burst out laughing, followed by Niall, Justin appeared relieved. "You had me going for a minute."

We got down to the serious task of eating, and Mick found a film to watch while we ate.

I have to admit, I really fell on my feet when I moved into this place. Like I said, we get along really well. There's only about five years' difference between the lot of us. Moz is the youngest, at twenty-five, and Mick's the oldest. He's thirty, and he's the steadying influence around the place. Not got much to say for himself, but he's got a sense of humour (as you've seen) and a level head in a crisis, like when the boiler went on the fritz in the middle of winter. Justin, for all his twenty-eight years, was flapping around like a headless chicken, but Mick calmly got it all sorted.

And now it looked like I'd found a confidante.

As if he'd read my mind, Niall glanced in my direction. He mouthed *okay?* and I gave him a nod. His quick flash of a smile made me feel good. Now all I had to worry about was what I was going to wear. I mean, what *do* you wear to go on a date with a gay man?

(I can hear you now. 'Clothes.' Not helping!)

I planned to spend most of Saturday going through my wardrobe, and if I didn't find anything that would knock Daniel's socks off, then I was going shopping for something that would. It wasn't until later that night that I thought about that. *Knock his socks off?* We were going to watch DVDs and eat takeaway. Why was I thinking so hard about how to impress him? He already thought I was cute, right? That had to be a good start.

Do I always go to this much trouble when I go on a date? Okay, so I'm no slob, but I'm not a fashion model either. Then it hit me. The way Daniel looked, he could easily be a model. Maybe I was feeling like I lacked a bit in the looks department. (Floppy hair, big chin, lips like a girl, remember?)

Oh God. I was thinking about him kissing me again. Sitting cuddled up together on his couch. Our eyes meeting over tiramisu and—

Tiramisu?

I needed to get a fucking grip. It was just a date. For all I knew, it was going to be a one-off. Maybe I'd spend an evening with Daniel and decide I wasn't up for another date.

But what if...?

Yeah. It was the *What if* that gave me butterflies.

Chapter 4

June 9, 2018

It was about six forty-five when I reached Daniel's flat. He hadn't been kidding—it was literally two minutes' walk from the station. The building looked fairly recent, with three stories and dormer windows set into the roof. There were a couple of doors into the place, so I searched for the one with Daniel's flat number. He was at the end of the block.

I paused at the door, staring at the intercom. Not that I was going to let him know I was there just yet. Fashionably late was one thing—a quarter of an hour early was quite another. He'd sent the takeaway menu along with his address, so dinner would probably be waiting for me.

Can't look as if I'm too eager, right?

"It's a bit late to change your mind now."

I almost jumped out of my skin. Daniel stood behind me, clutching a large brown paper bag with a handle. He was smiling.

And fuck, he looked good. Tight jeans that could have been sprayed on, a pair of black Skechers, and a light blue hoodie. He wasn't wearing make-up this time, but trust me, he didn't need to—his face was still stunningly pretty.

"I hate being early," I said by way of explanation. Then I sniffed up. "Oh wow. That smells wonderful."

"I just collected it. I thought I had enough time to get back here before you arrived." Daniel chuckled. "I guess I should've known what time the train gets in from Reading." He reached into his pocket for a set of keys, then paused. "Well… are you going to stand there and wait for seven o'clock, or are you going to come in with me?"

I rolled my eyes. "Oh, I don't know. Let me think about it."

He laughed. "Well, while *you* think about it, *I'll* go upstairs and eat all the garlic and rosemary focaccia." I might have whimpered at that part, and he shook his head, murmuring, "You really are cute."

Daniel opened the door and I followed him inside. It turned out his flat was on the top floor, taking up one end of the building.

"I was going to collect the food then get ready," he said as we climbed the stairs.

"You mean you're not ready now? You could've fooled me." I wasn't just being polite.

He turned his head to glance at me. "You're great for my ego." We reached his floor, and he put the key in the lock. "It's not a big flat," he said as he let us into it.

I chuckled. "Trust me, it's bigger than my

place. I have a room to call my own, and it's that small, you couldn't swing the proverbial cat in it." We stepped into a light hallway, with five doors leading off it.

Daniel gestured to the first door on the left. "Important things first. That's the bathroom. Except it doesn't have a bath." He paused, studying me. "You look good."

I waved a hand, as if I always spent four hours deciding what to wear, then an hour in front of the mirror trying to get my hair to look less floppy and more done-this-way-on-purpose. In the end, I'd gone for my jeans *without* the trendy ripped knees, and my favourite smart shirt in a soft, dark blue fabric, open at the collar. I carried my plain black jacket. Not too dressy, neat, and simple.

"I'm glad you came," Daniel said quietly. Then he bit his lip. "Are you going to think me forward if I kiss you on the cheek?"

Oh God. My heartbeat sped up a little. "That depends. Do you greet all your guests like that?"

He chuckled. "Pretty much."

My pulse racing, I proffered my cheek. "Then go for it." I held my breath as he moved closer, his lips brushing softly against my skin.

He stepped back, his eyes twinkling. "You can breathe now." Yeah, there was that amused tone again.

I exhaled, aware that I was trembling

slightly.

Daniel hesitated, almost as if he was debating saying something, then headed for the second door on the left. "Let me dish all this out. The living room is the door dead ahead. The dinner table's in there too. You've got a few minutes before I'll be ready, so take a look around the place." He turned to face me, smirking. "That should take all of ten seconds." Then he disappeared into the kitchen.

I took a moment to let my heart calm the fuck down. *It was just a peck on the cheek, for God's sake.* I went to the door at the end of the hallway and pushed it open. The living room took up a corner of the flat, with dormer windows on two sides. It was an uncluttered room, with only a corner sofa with chaise end, a low coffee table in front of it, a table and four chairs, a cream-coloured desk below one window, and a TV set at an angle in the corner. The hardwood floor looked like oak.

I removed my jacket and placed it over the back of a dining chair. The room had a cosy feel to it. I wanted to see the rest of the flat, but seeing as there were only bedrooms left, I decided against it. Looking at his bedroom felt wrong, almost like I was checking it out for later.

And what if we end up there?

Okay, this really wasn't me. I've fucked on the first date, sure, but I've also been on dates which ended with a peck on the cheek and a 'thank you for a lovely evening.' And for me to be this nervous about the prospect of ending up in Daniel's bed… Yeah. *So* not like me.

It's just sex, right? I mean, how different can it be? I know what goes where, yeah? And that soft brushing of lips against my cheek…

"Have you finished the tour already?" Daniel asked from the doorway. In his hand was a long dish filled with fragrant focaccia.

"I gave the bedrooms a miss."

He chuckled. "It's okay. I tidied up before you arrived." His eyes sparkled. "Anything that might frighten the horses is safely out of sight."

I arched my eyebrows. "The mind boggles."

He laughed and placed the dish on the table. "Seeing as I'm having chicken and you're having mushrooms, I thought a bottle of white wine might be nice. That's if you drink wine."

"I drink anything." Then I stilled, aware of how that sounded. "Well, I mean, I like wine, and—"

"It's okay, I get the picture."

It was then I noticed that he'd taken off the hoodie. Daniel wore a pale pink top with a low scoop neckline, and barely-there sleeves that were tight around his slightly toned upper arms. The top clung everywhere it touched, come to think of it, including his nipples that pushed against the fabric, tight enough for me to tell they were pierced.

Okay. *No part* of me is pierced. Or tattooed.

That might be because I'm not a fan of needles. As in, I did faint once when I had to give blood, but only because I looked when the nurse said not to. And was it *fuck* 'a sharp scratch.'

"Do you want to see them?"

Oh God. I'd been staring at his nipples.

I coughed loudly, trying my best not to say, 'yes please.' Because while *I* might not have the slightest desire to mutilate my body, that didn't mean I was averse to staring at someone *else's* body art. And I really did want to see how they looked.

"I must've zoned out," I said quickly once I'd stopped coughing.

"Mm-hmm." Daniel's lips twitched. "Well, take a seat. Dinner's coming." Then he left me alone again.

I pulled out a chair and sat, my heart pounding, trying not to think about what kind of impression I was giving. I picked up a piece of focaccia, inhaling its garlicky goodness.

Shit. Garlic. *Well, fuck*. That was kissing Daniel off the menu then. Except… he'd be eating it too. *That works, right?*

Great. Right then I was cursing myself for not bringing along a toothbrush and some mint toothpaste.

Daniel returned with two plates, and the aroma was heavenly. He put them on the table, then went off to get the wine. By the time he was seated, and the wine poured, my heartbeat had returned to normal.

He raised his glass. “To our first date.”

I didn’t know how to respond, because part of me was dying to know if there was going to be a second, but I didn’t dare ask. Instead, I raised my glass and clicked it against his, and then we set to eating.

Daniel was right about the food. It was extremely good. My fettuccine in a wild mushroom sauce was delicious, and his chicken fillet down in a creamy lemon sauce was making my mouth water. Obviously, he noticed my drool, because he cut off a piece of the chicken, dipped it into the sauce, and held out his fork to me.

“Try it?”

As if I was going to say no.

He fed it to me, and I held onto the fork in my mouth just a fraction longer than I needed to. (Okay, yes, I was flirting. So what? I was on a date, wasn’t I?) Daniel widened his eyes a little, and his lips parted.

Score one to me for successful flirting.

“So tell me about these guys you share a house with.” He grinned. “When you said that, I had visions of The Young Ones. You know, that comedy from the eighties they repeat now and again? Four students, blowing up stuff, things growing in the fridge, permanent chaos…”

I laughed. I hadn’t seen it, but I could

imagine. "Nothing would dare grow in our fridge. Niall would bleach it to death."

"Is Niall a clean freak?"

"He's a baker," I explained. "And we're a bit old to be students. Even if Justin still acts like one." I told him about my housemates, their habits, the laughs we'd shared.

"Let's change the subject," he said after a while.

"What do you want to talk about?"

"You." Daniel refilled our glasses.

And there went my heartbeat again, picking up speed. "What do you want to know?"

He gave me a sheepish glance that was adorable. "Your age? Because you've got this fresh-faced look about you, and I don't have a clue how old you are. You could be eighteen for all I know."

"Oh, and you talk about me being good for *your* ego?" I smiled. "I'm twenty-six." I gazed at him expectantly.

"Twenty-seven. And you're single."

My throat tightened a little, and I eased it with a sip of wine. "Yes." I didn't want to talk about me. "Is there dessert? I don't think you mentioned that."

Daniel chuckled, and I had the sneaking suspicion he'd seen right through me. "There's a raspberry cheesecake in the fridge, and vanilla ice cream."

I couldn't help myself. "No tiramisu?"

He arched his eyebrows. "They don't do tiramisu at Mio Fiore. At least, it's not on the takeaway menu."

"Sounds great," I assured him, and he got up from the table to fetch it. I took advantage of his absence to breathe deeply. Flirting with him over a mouthful of chicken fillet was one thing. Answering questions that might reveal more than I was prepared for was another.

I'm not doing anything wrong, I reminded myself. *It's just dinner and a DVD*. Then why was my stomach tied up in perpetual knots? Daniel was a nice guy. He was funny, intelligent, and gorgeous. So what if he was gay? That didn't mean anything had to happen between us, did it?

Yeah. For some reason my brain had lost the purpose of a date.

Daniel returned with the dessert, and the rest of the meal passed without incident. When we were finished, Daniel collected the dishes and took them to the kitchen. He returned to the living room, picked up the half bottle of wine that remained, and gestured to the sofa. "Ready for our film?"

A film? Sure. Anything else? I had no idea.

I sat in the middle of the sofa, while Daniel grabbed the DVD and fed it into the player. He walked over to the sofa and glanced down at me. "You can sit here if you want," he said, pointing to the chaise end. "Make yourself comfy."

I could do that.

I shifted my arse across, then settled against the cushions. Daniel sat beside me, aimed the remote at the TV, and then dropped it onto the seat cushions at the other end of the sofa.

I'll be honest. I can't tell you anything that happened in the first ten minutes of the film. I was too busy wondering what was coming up. Gradually, however, the hamster in my head stopped flying around on its little wheel, my heart decided to resume its normal rhythm, and I relaxed enough to enjoy the film.

Something else Daniel was right about—it was a brilliant film. It was funny, especially the bits where the hero, Hiccup, used sneaky tricks to win over the dragons without violence. The idea of someone tickling a dragon to subdue him made me laugh out loud, and Daniel was laughing right along with me. I don't think I stopped smiling the whole time the film was on, except for when Hiccup fell. Without thinking, I gripped the nearest thing to me—which happened to be Daniel's thigh. No sooner had my fingers encountered firmness, than I pulled away, embarrassed.

Daniel chuckled. "No harm done. Wait till we're watching a horror film. I'll be holding onto you the whole time. I'm a wuss when it comes to scary movies." Then he went back to watching the film.

The casual remark told me two things.

Daniel intended for there to be more than one date, and by the sound of it, touching would be involved.

Despite my earlier nerves, I had no problem with either. The film had been just that—a film—and I hadn't minded that a bit. I was comfortable, relaxed, and I was enjoying myself. I'd drunk half a bottle of white wine, which meant I wasn't drunk, but delightfully muzzy.

The credits rolled at the end and I sighed happily. "That was great."

"Well, we've got How To Train Your Dragon 2 still to come, if you want to watch it."

I did a mental assessment. It was almost nine thirty. I'd checked on train times, and the last one left Newbury at eleven thirty-eight. There was time enough for another film.

If I wanted to stay.

"I could do," I began, but before I could finish, Daniel stopped my words with his fingers to my lips.

"Are you going to stop me if I try to kiss you?" His gaze met mine. "Because God knows, I've wanted to do that all evening."

I glanced at his lips, so pink and soft-looking. Hell, I *knew* they were soft. My heart was racing again, blood was pounding in my ears, and I was shivering. Not from fear, or apprehension.

From desire.

"Then kiss me," I whispered, swallowing hard.

Daniel shifted, his hand going around to the back of my neck as he pulled me down into a gentle kiss. No tongue, just lips, and *fuck*, it felt amazing. My body grew warm, and it was as if every tiny sound was amplified, from the low hum of the DVD player to the clock on the wall as it ticked away the passing seconds. My hand was on his neck, stroking him there. I shivered again, but this time with pleasure.

Then he broke the kiss and sat back, his eyes shining, his breathing quick. "Wow."

I swallowed again. "Is that a good wow or a bad wow?"

Daniel smiled. "It was a 'if this is how you kiss, I can't wait to get you into bed' wow."

Oh my God. He said the B word.

I fought to breathe and managed to croak one word. It was supposed to be wow, but that wasn't what came out.

"Whoa."

Chapter 5

I was so full of shit, wasn't I?

All this talk of being open to dating a guy, thinking about kissing Daniel, flirting with him… but when push came to shove, I was trembling like a leaf.

And all he'd done was kiss me.

"Lee. *Lee.*"

I blinked, and there I was, back in Daniel's flat, Daniel beside me on the sofa, gazing at me with—

Warmth. A touch of confusion. And then… comprehension.

I drew in a deep breath. "Sorry about that."

Daniel shifted away from me, not much, but enough to send a signal.

He's changed his mind. He doesn't want to date me. I've fucked it up. Despite my self-loathing for reacting the way I had, it still came down to this: I did *not* want to fuck this up.

"Something you want to tell me?" Daniel gave me an inquiring glance. When I said nothing, he gave a slow nod, his eyes still warm. "Okay. I'll tell you, shall I? You said you hadn't been out with a guy before. I took that to mean you're only recently out, or you've just worked out you're gay, but… that's not it at all, is it?" He didn't break eye contact.

All I could do was shake my head.

"You're straight." It wasn't a question, so I didn't answer. Daniel nodded, as though he'd expected that. "Can I ask you something? Why did you say yes when I asked you out? Am I some sort of… experiment?"

Aw fuck.

Before I could respond, he expelled a long breath. "There's something you should know about me. I don't usually go around asking complete strangers I meet on a train for a date. In fact, I'd *never* done that—until I met you." His dark brown eyes locked onto mine. "And even now, I'm not sure why I asked you."

"There was *something*, wasn't there?" I blurted out. "At least, there was for me. When we shook hands. And… and the way you looked at me."

"You liked it."

I nodded. "No one has ever… I mean, I'd never even *thought* about…" I was lost for words.

Daniel stretched out his hand toward me, as if to stroke my cheek, but checked himself at the last minute and withdrew it. "I'm not going to be your little sexual experiment, Lee," he said quietly.

"That's not what I want, honest," I said at once. Except I wasn't sure what I wanted right then.

Daniel regarded me thoughtfully. "Okay. This is what we're gonna do. I'm going to end this date right now."

My heart sank. "Okay."

He was still looking at me. "You're going to go home. But you *can* come back."

I stilled. *What?*

Daniel's breathing quickened. "Only if you're serious about continuing where we left off, and *only* after you've given it a lot of thought."

I didn't understand. Then I noticed he was shaking, and my heart pounded.

"I think you could be someone special," he said at last. "I felt as much on the train."

Fuck, my heart was going so fast. *I felt the same way*, I wanted to shout. But Daniel wasn't finished.

"If you decide you want to pursue this—and everything *this* entails… if this is what you *really* want, then come find me."

I knew what he was talking about. *This* meant more dates. Sex. Daniel was simply laying his cards on the table, making sure I knew right from the start.

Making sure I knew what I was letting myself in for—*if* I came back.

"Okay," I said in as firm a voice as I could manage. "Just…" I swallowed. "I never meant to mess you around."

Daniel's smile was more of a reassurance than his words. "I know. And I'm not a one-night stand kind of guy. I don't do lots of hook-ups. I only make a move if something about a person speaks to me." He met my gaze. "Like you did." He got to his feet and went over to the chair where I'd left my jacket. "Thank you for a lovely evening," he said as he handed it to me.

"I should be thanking you. The food and the DVD were great." The kiss had been pretty amazing too. Our hands touched as I took the jacket, and I shivered. "Daniel, I—"

He raised his hand and stopped my words for the second time that evening. "Don't. Please?"

I nodded, and he slowly removed his fingers from my lips. He walked me to his front door and opened it. "Text me when you're home? Just so I know you got there?"

God, it was such a sweet thing to say.

"I will."

"And… you can text me anytime you like. Call me, if you want. Whatever. But don't come back here unless you're serious."

Impulsively, I leaned in and kissed his cheek. "Thank you," I whispered, before stepping out onto the landing. I didn't look back as I headed down the stairs, my heart hammering.

I had a train to catch and a lot of thinking to do.

#LoveWins
love is love

Sunday went by in a haze. I don't remember much about it. My mind kept defaulting to Daniel—his kiss, his words, his hand on my neck, the way he'd looked at me… I kept recalling the hurt in his eyes when he asked if he was my experiment.

Yeah. That had stung. Because I could see how he might think that.

I must have seemed distracted because the others gave me a wide berth. Niall went out God knew where, Justin was in his room listening to music very loudly for most of the day, and Moz vegged out on the couch watching TV. There was no sign of Mick, so I assumed he was escaping us in his room on the top floor.

I got my work clothes ready for the week ahead, but I could do that on autopilot. By Sunday evening, I was sitting on my bed, deep in thought.

What would be so bad about dating Daniel?

Well, there was one obvious answer, one that didn't make me like myself very much. *What would people say?* And by 'people' I meant my housemates and my parents. I didn't give a shit what that bunch of fuckwits at work thought, because whoever I was dating was none of their fucking business. The housemates, though… I'd have to tell them. I already knew Niall would have my back. One down, three to go…

Listen to yourself. You're already talking like it's a done deal and you're working out how to tell them you're gay.

Except that was the problem. I didn't think I was gay. I didn't *feel* gay.

What I *did* feel was confused at fuck.

A soft knocking on my door brought me down to earth. "Come in." I gave the room a quick glance. It was tidy, thank God.

(Hey, I don't want them thinking I'm a slob!)

Mick poked his head around the door. "You got a minute?"

I chuckled. "I think I can fit you into my jam-packed schedule."

He came into the room and closed the door behind him. For a moment, he stood looking awkwardly around. There was only one chair, and I sure wouldn't sit on it. The damn thing was only good for putting stuff on. I gestured to the end of the bed. "Park yourself there."

Mick sat, leaning against the footboard. "You've been awfully quiet today. I got worried."

I stared at him. "Just because I was quiet?"

"Actually, more because of what I heard between you and Niall on Friday when you got home."

I sat very still. "You were listening?"

"The lounge windows were open. So were the kitchen windows." He shrugged. "What can I say? Your voices carried. And yeah, I *could've* gone to my room and worked there, but once you started talking, I had to hear the rest."

"Why?" I demanded. I'd always liked Mick. He was a solid reliable guy, but *this*….

Mick didn't reply but took his phone from his pocket. He scrolled across the screen before handing it to me. I took it and gazed at a photo of him and another guy.

What stopped me dead in my tracks was the fact that the guy had his arms around Mick. And that I'd never seen Mick look so… happy. Then I took another look at the guy. *He looks pretty.*

Okay, he reminded me of Daniel.

I put two and two together. "You're gay?" He'd never said a *word.*

To my surprise, Mick shook his head.

I sagged against the pillows. "You're making my head hurt. None of this makes any sense. You don't go out. You don't date. You're either at the hospital or you're here. So how can you have a boyfriend?"

"You know those IT management courses they send me on every three months?" Mick's eye twinkled. "There are no such courses. Well… there *are*… I just haven't been on one in a long time."

I gaped. "That's when you… but… only

every three months? Where does he live?"

"Edinburgh." Mick held out his hand for his phone, then pocketed it. "I suppose I'd better tell you the whole story. You need to hear it anyway, because it's relevant to your situation."

Okay, now I was truly intrigued.

"I've known him for years. We were at uni together."

The affectionate look in his eyes made me smile. "Did you fancy him then?"

Mick chuckled. "No, not then. I wasn't into men. I knew he was gay though. We used to go out for a drink on a Saturday night. I'd tell him about my dating successes or disasters, and he'd tell me about his. Once we left uni, we stayed in touch. Anyway, about three years ago, I went up to Scotland to see him, and he was in a state. He'd recently broken up with his fiancé. We went out on the town and got drunk." He chuckled again. "I think you can guess what happened next."

I gave a mock gasp. "He was on the rebound. He had his wicked way with you."

Mick burst into laughter. "Sorry to disappoint you, but I was the one who initiated it. *He* kept stopping to make sure I was okay with everything we were doing. So no, he didn't take advantage of his poor drunken straight friend."

"Then what happened?"

"I woke up the next morning in his bed, both of us starkers, empty condom packets on the floor, and neither of us able to look the other in the eye. Once we'd got some coffee down our necks, we went out and had breakfast, then we came back to his flat and talked, which was the best thing we could've done."

"And you've been together ever since?"

Mick nodded. "But this is the point I'm trying to make. I don't fancy guys. I never did. Just him. He was the one person with whom I had a connection. It didn't matter that up till then, I'd only ever shagged women." He sighed. "It didn't stop him being afraid at first. He thought I was going to come to my senses, and remember I liked women and leave him."

"What's his name?" It felt odd talking about Mick's anonymous boyfriend.

"Pete."

One thing puzzled me. "How can you say you're not gay if you have a boyfriend?"

"I suppose because I hate labels. I just happen to be in a long-distance relationship with a guy."

"A guy you've never mentioned before."

Mick arched his eyebrows. "That would be because it's no one's business but mine."

"So, not because you don't want us knowing you're gay."

He shook his head. "And there you go again with the labels. I think it's easier for me to say what I'm *not* rather than what I am."

I blinked. “What does that mean?”

Mick counted off on his fingers. “I’m *not* a closeted gay man who fears being gay. I’m *not* tired of sex with women. I’m *not* frustrated by a lack of success with women. I *don’t* think of myself as bi.”

“Why not bi?”

Mick shrugged. “I think that’s just me nit-picking. Bisexuality implies attraction to both males and females, and I’m only interested in one male in particular. The rest of the male species don’t do a thing for me.” He grinned. “Sorry, sweetheart, that includes you too.”

I brought my hand to my forehead in a dramatic gesture. “I’ll try not to be offended,” I said with a heavy sigh. Mick chuckled. “Okay, so if you’re not all those things, what does that leave?”

He smiled. “A man who made a connection with, and fell in love with, another man. Which brings me to why I’m sitting on your bed right now.” He folded his arms. “What about you?”

“What about me?”

Mick gazed at me thoughtfully. “Let me ask you a few questions. Could you be attracted to a guy? Could you have sex with a guy? Would you consider having a relationship with a guy?”

I swallowed. Hadn’t I been asking myself the same questions ever since I met Daniel? “Maybe… if I really liked him.”

Mick nodded. "Now, if someone put those questions to someone of my *grandad's* age, they'd probably get the response of 'Absolutely not!' But you and me, we're a different generation, and times are changing. Sexuality is much more… fluid. Which brings me back to you and this… Daniel, is that his name?" I nodded. "Okay, let's talk about you and Daniel. What I remember most about your conversation with Niall, was the whole 'but I'm straight' scenario." He leaned forward, his eyes bright. "Stop shoving yourself into a box. Go with how you *feel*." He cocked his head to one side. "How did the date go?"

I took a breath, and it all tumbled out of me in a rush of words and emotions. Mick listened, not speaking, just nodding, his gazed focused on my face. When I was done, I breathed more easily.

Finally, Mick spoke. "That's what you've been doing all day, isn't it? Thinking."

"Yeah. I don't think I came to any conclusions." Well, I *hadn't*, but that was before Mick came to sit on my bed and completely changed my view of him. There was one question I'd been dying to ask, however. "Does your family know? About Pete, I mean?"

"Yeah." His face tightened. "I'm not going to lie. That was the hardest part about all of this. But I have to say, they're getting better about it." He gave a sad smile. "I've just had to… re-educate them."

And there it was, the worry that had niggled away at the back of my mind, always there, always dripping doubt and uncertainty into my thoughts. "I might ask you how you did that."

Mick stared at me. "Ah. I get it. You're thinking about how your family is going to react to Daniel."

I nodded. Then I realized I'd admitted to more than my concerns.

Mick had caught it though. "Then you *are* going to pursue this?"

"Yes. Because all those things you're *not*?" I smiled. "I'm not those either. And the way you look when you talk about Pete? I want to feel like that about someone." Because I hadn't even felt like that about Cheryl, and *how* long had we dated for? A year?

Mick got off the bed, and I stood too. "Any time you want to talk, you know where I am, okay? But do me a favour? The best person you can talk to about the way you're feeling is not me, or Niall—it's Daniel."

"He said I could call or text him."

"Then do that." Mick gave me a hug. "And something else to think about. Half this house now knows you're interested in a guy. That only leaves Justin and Moz." He grinned. "As if you'd give a shit what Justin thinks."

He had a point.

Mick walked over to the door. "Let me

know what you decide to do." His eyes twinkled. "Not that I don't already have an idea."

That glint in his eyes reminded me of something. "Er, Mick? Those… gadgets you were talking about on Friday night…"

Mick's lips twitched. "No, you can't borrow them. Buy your own." He grinned. "But I'll show you where to find them." Then he was gone, closing the door behind him.

It only took a second for his meaning to penetrate.

OMG. He was talking about sex toys. Toys for boys.

Yeah, we were going to talk about that. But first I had to talk to Daniel, and there was no time like the present.

Chapter 6

Hey Daniel? You okay to talk?

Seconds later my phone burst into life, and I smiled. Apparently, he was. I stretched out on the bed and got comfortable. "Hi."

"So how was *your* day?"

Okay, that made me laugh. "I didn't do much. I had something on my mind."

"Yeah. I know the feeling." Daniel's voice softened. "Please don't think I was being mean when I ended things the way I did. To be honest, I moved too fast, kissing you like that."

"Do you usually kiss on the first date?" I was genuinely interested. I'd known girls who were happy with that, a few who'd looked at me like I'd stuck my hand up their skirt, and one bold woman who'd felt me up in the taxi back to her place.

Not that I'd complained, mind you.

"Honey, I've *fucked* on the first date. Though that's a rarity."

So we weren't *that* dissimilar. "What did you do today?"

"I worked my arse off, actually. We were rehearsing for next month."

"Rehearsing? For what? Are you an actor too?"

Daniel chuckled. "No, although I was a member of a local theatre group a few years back. Now I'm part of a gay male dance troupe. We're getting ready for Pride."

"The parade in London?" Not that I'd ever seen it except on TV. I didn't go anywhere near London on Pride day.

"So we've heard of Pride, then?"

I knew a mocking tone when I heard it. "Yeah, yeah, take the piss out of the straight boy." Fuck, Mick was right. Me and labels.

"You could come watch us. You'd get to see me in my purple lycra, brandishing a whopping great rainbow flag. Oh, and my high-heeled boots."

Okay, I'm gonna be honest here. He said lycra, and my mind went instantly to a lithe Daniel wearing something that resembled a second skin, leaving nothing to the imagination. Then his words sank in. *High-heeled boots?*

Apparently, my dick liked the sound of that.

Yeah. Not so straight after all.

I cleared my throat. "I've never been to Pride."

"Why not? It's a lot of fun."

"Well… because… I never saw the point?"

Daniel laughed. "Honey, you don't have to be gay to watch a Pride parade. People go to support friends, family, and complete strangers who are LGBTQA."

"What does the Q stand for? And the A?" I felt like an idiot. I should know this stuff, right?

Daniel sighed. "I can see I've got some work to do with you, haven't I?" Before I could respond, his voice grew warmer. "Isn't it a good thing that I think you're worth the effort?"

"Yeah?" There was sudden heat in my chest, and a pleasurable feeling of lightness all over my body. And right then I wanted him to know I *was* worth it. "Did you ever see that film, Hitchhiker's Guide to the Galaxy?"

"I prefer the books, but yeah."

"You know the bit when they change the description of the Earth to 'Mostly harmless'? Well… I think I've come up with a new sexuality." My heartbeat quickened. "'Mostly Straight.' I like to think of it as straight with a dash of gayness."

Daniel let out another warm chuckle. "This sounds encouraging. Only a dash though? How much is a dash? Are we talking a mere sprinkling, or a hefty dollop?"

I took a deep breath. "I don't think there's a set amount. It's kind of… fluid."

A pause. "Then this does sound encouraging. I'd like to see how it develops." Another pause. "Is it likely to develop?"

I knew what he was asking. "I think so." Daniel wanted me not to go into this half-cocked, as it were, so I *was* going to think about it.

"Do you like dancing?"

I laughed. "Not sure you could compare what *I* do with *your* efforts, but yeah, I have been known to make some moves down on a dance floor." Usually where I didn't know anyone and didn't give a shit who saw me.

Okay, so what if my sister says I look like a duck waddling when I dance? What the fuck would she know? The last time she saw me dance, I was *six years old*, for God's sake.

I rest my case.

"I'd like to see you dance," Daniel said in a low voice. "I bet you're a lovely mover."

This time there was no doubt in my mind. "You're flirting with me."

"Says you. I can spot flirting too. And there was *definite* flirting going on last Friday on the train."

"Okay. Guilty."

"I didn't mind," Daniel added. Then he yawned.

I chuckled. "Is that a comment on my conversation technique?"

"I'm sorry, I'm just exhausted. It was a long rehearsal and we had a lot to sort out. I should be thinking about bed, to be honest. Got to make sure I'm awake to get that train, right?"

I snorted. "You and me both." Most mornings it was definitely a case of mind over mattress. "I'd better let you sleep then."

"Are you going to be thinking about me this week?"

If Sunday was anything to go by, Daniel was going to be on my mind a lot in the coming days. "Yes."

"Oh." It was amazing how happy one little word could sound, and that made *me* happy too. "Goodnight, then."

"Goodnight. Sweet dreams."

Daniel's chuckle filled my ears. "Oh, they'll be sweet. I'll be dreaming of you, cutie." And then he disconnected.

I tossed my phone aside onto the bed and stared at the ceiling.

He still wants me.

He's still interested.

I felt like a teenager all over again, and fuck, it felt good.

I got ready for bed, climbed between the sheets and reached over to switch off the lamp. My last thought before I fell asleep was to wonder if I'd see him on the train the next day.

I hoped so.

#LoveWins

love is love

When I got home Monday night, thankfully there was no one around to see the plastic bag I was clutching. I made it up to my room without seeing a soul and closed the door. Then I kicked off my shoes, took off my jacket, and changed into a pair of shorts and a T-shirt.

Daniel hadn't been on the 18.04, and part of me had been disappointed by that. I told myself it was just timing that had connected us on Friday, that he could take any number of trains to get home. When I found myself looking up trains that carried on from Reading to Newbury, I got my first glimpse of how important Daniel was becoming to me.

I debated calling him, but I had nothing new to tell him. *Better to call him when I have something to say.* Besides, I had something to do.

The portable DVD player Mum had got me for Christmas a few years ago stood on the shelf, its black case gathering dust. I grabbed it, sneezed twice, and unzipped it.

The knock at the door nearly gave me a heart attack. "I'm busy!" I called out.

Niall chuckled. "Oops. Shall I come back when you're finished?"

"Get in here." When he poked his head cautiously around the door, I glared at him. "I hope no one else is around to hear you say that."

"So what if they are? They'll just think you're having a wank and you want privacy." Niall grinned. “At least you closed the door. Justin doesn’t bother. He leaves his wide open while he’s pulling his pud.” Justin’s room was right next to the bathroom. Going for a piss could be entertaining at times.

Niall peered at the bed. “Someone’s been shopping in HMV, I see. What have you been buying?”

I sighed. “Close the door.” Niall did as instructed, then came and sat on the bed, gazing at the bag with obvious interest. I grabbed the bottom corners, tipped it up, and a DVD spilled out onto the duvet.

Niall picked it up, staring at the cover. “Queer as Folk,” he read aloud. He blinked.

“Call it research.”

He smirked. “No shit.” He read the back of the box in silence. “Ooh. This sounds good. Can I watch it with you?”

I glared at him. “No, you can *not*.”

“Aw, why not?”

“I was going to watch it with my earbuds, and there’s only one socket.”

Niall’s eyes gleamed. “I’ve got a Y-Splitter. You plug it in, and two people can listen at the same time.”

He wasn’t going to back down. “Fine. After we’ve eaten.”

“Or maybe we could watch the first episode now?”

I simply stared at him.

He put it down, then regarded me with a quizzical glance. "What made you get it?"

I wasn't sure myself. I'd wandered into HMV during my lunch hour and found myself at the Gay and Lesbian section of the DVD department. I could have spent a *lot* of money in there, because every DVD I picked up grabbed my interest. I'd finally settled on this one, rather than the US version, because I recognized the director, Russell T. Davies, from his work on Doctor Who. Not that I was expecting anything like *that*.

As for why… Maybe I wanted to know Daniel better, and I thought this series was a way to understand him.

I remember being seventeen and still living with my parents, when Brokeback Mountain was shown on TV. It got to the part when Jake Gyllenhaal was in the tent with Heath Ledger, and my Mum grabbed the remote and changed channels, muttering something like, 'well, I don't think we need to see *that*.' Dad murmured in agreement before glancing across at me.

Looking back now, that glance could be interpreted in a couple of ways. He didn't want his son 'corrupted', or he wanted to see if I was taking more than a reasonable amount of interest in it. Sadly, knowing my dad, either of those might have been the correct one.

I can still recall how disappointed I was,

especially the following day in sixth form college, when everyone was talking about it. Maybe it was me, but I couldn't remember seeing many gay characters on TV programmes when I was growing up. Now they were everywhere, but in the early noughties, not so much.

I knew there was another reason for buying Queer as Folk, and that reason was sex. The cover made it obvious there was going to be fucking, and I wanted to see something that wasn't porn.

Yeah. About that.

I'm not going to lie. I watch porn, okay? (Hey, if I said I was a twenty-six-year-old male who'd never watched a porno in his life, you'd be rolling your eyes in a millisecond.) It's great for rubbing one off, but it's not real, is it? That girl isn't moaning because he's the best fuck she's ever had—it's because whoever was behind the camera told her to make it loud.

The director of Queer as Folk was a British gay man, so it stood to reason the series would reflect gay men—I hoped. I wanted to find some common ground with Daniel, some way to get an insight into what he wanted, how he thought…

I didn't have a fucking clue.

I realized I hadn't answered Niall's question. "I'm not really sure why I bought it, to be honest." I smiled. "But you're right. It looks good." I deliberately moved the DVD out of his reach. "Later."

"Fine. In that case, I'm going to get something to eat. I'll be back."

I chuckled. "Yes, Arnie." I waited till he'd left the room before picking up the DVD.

This was going to be interesting.

#lovewins
love is love

You know how sometimes you realize way too late that you *really* shouldn't have said yes?

Yup. That was me, when I found myself sitting next to Niall on my bed, the pair of us staring at the screen of my DVD player, where two naked men were in a bed together. One lay face down, propped up on his elbows, while the other licked a line up his spine. Then he moved lower and did it again. Lower. Lower, until—

"Jesus," I muttered. I mean, I'd seen rimming before, so why was this so different?

Because I didn't expect to find it in a TV series, and somehow that made it *way* hotter. We only saw the main character with the guy's legs up on his shoulders, and the scene ended there, but my imagination did the rest. When the first episode ended, I hit Stop and removed my earbuds.

Niall seemed totally unfazed by it. Then I remembered—he'd watched gay porn. He pulled his earbuds free and gazed at me expectantly. "Well?"

I coughed. "I can see it's going to give me something to talk about when I next see Daniel."

"I was going to ask about that. The last I heard, you'd called him. Did you go on that date? How did it go?" Niall frowned. "You were really quiet yesterday, and I didn't want to say anything, in case it had gone badly."

I told him what had happened, apart from the kissing part. Some things are not for sharing, okay?

"So will you see him again?"

I think I'd already decided on that after the talk with Mick. "Yeah, I think so."

Niall nodded slowly. "Good for you. And I hope it works out for you." He gestured to the DVD box. "Can I borrow it when you've watched them all?"

I laughed. "Yeah, of course." Besides, I wasn't sure it was the accurate representation I'd expected. All gay men couldn't be like that—could they? I thought about Daniel, his quiet insistence that he wasn't into one-night stands and hook-ups. He was streets away from the brash and sexually predatory Stuart from the DVD.

Maybe real life is what I need, not someone's fantasy.

Chapter 7

June 15, 2018

I walked despondently along the platform, heading for the front coach as usual.

There'd been no sign of Daniel all week.

I'd scanned the station concourse every night, hoping to catch a glimpse of him. Throngs of commuters, yes, but no Daniel. I'd waited until the last minute before boarding the train, in case I spied him on the platform, but no luck.

Yes, I know I could've called him, but…

(Do you think it's a British 'thing', not wanting to be a pain in the arse? I think so. I think it's a part of us, the same part that apologizes when someone bumps into *us,* rather than the other way around. Bloody hell, we're an apologetic race.)

I got onto the coach and headed for the seats at the front. I wasn't bothered about a table, because all I was going to do was close my eyes until we reached Reading. The air con was working, thank goodness, because it had been a warm day. I took off my jacket and threw it up on the parcel shelf, undid the top three buttons of my shirt, and plonked myself down in the window seat, dumping my bag on the empty seat beside me.

I'll call him tonight.

I was going to call him anyway. Five days since we'd last spoken, and all I could do was think about him. I watched some talent show, and a male dancer came onto the stage, moving rhythmically to the music.

I thought of Daniel.

Walking toward Paddington Station on Thursday evening, I'd caught a glimpse of a pretty male face, with pink, glistening lips, high cheekbones, and purple eye shadow, his head crowned with highlighted hair.

My heart had skipped a beat, until I got closer and realized it wasn't him.

"Is this seat taken?"

I glanced up at the speaker, and damn it, there went my heart into its stuttering routine again. Daniel stood there, looking gorgeous in a white shirt and pale blue jacket over his jeans. His lips bore a trace of gloss, and his eyes were accentuated by eye liner.

He was smiling.

I grabbed my bag and yanked it out of the way for him.

Daniel laughed and sat, his own bag on his knee. "I'll take that as a no." He half-turned his body toward me. "Hello there."

"I've missed you this week," I blurted out. "I looked for you every evening."

"I know. I saw you."

I frowned. "You—where were you? I didn't see you."

"That's because I stayed out of sight."

I guess my expression registered my hurt because his face fell.

"I wanted to give you space. I realized after we spoke on Sunday that I wasn't playing fair." Daniel rested his head against the highbacked seat. "I *was* flirting with you, and I had no right to do that, not when I'd asked you to think carefully and weigh up everything. And when I didn't hear from you again, I thought I'd pushed too hard." He sighed. "It's been such an effort to stay away from you this week."

"But you're here now." And I was reading a hell of a lot into that.

The train lurched forward, and the computer-generated voice welcomed us aboard the train. All I could think of was that I had nineteen minutes with him before I had to get off the train.

"Is there something wrong with my mouth?"

I blinked. "Excuse me?"

Daniel appeared amused. "My mouth. You're staring at it."

Damn it. I thought quickly. "Is that lip gloss you're wearing? Doesn't it wear off during the day?"

He leaned in and whispered conspiratorially, "I reapply before I leave the shop.

A guy's got to look fabulous on the train, right?" His eyes sparkled. "You never know who you'll run into." He leaned back. "How was work this week? Any more dealings with She with the face like a slapped arse?"

I groaned. "Don't remind me. On Wednesday she told me I needed to work on my sincerity when I was answering calls. I'm sorry, but sounding sincere when you're dealing with a guy who's rung up because his new monitor isn't working, and then you discover he hasn't even plugged the bloody thing in…"

Daniel chuckled. "Do you get many calls like that?"

"You have no idea. The best one was yesterday. This hysterical woman calls me, asking how she can open up her vacuum cleaner, because it's just sucked up her hamster that was running around on the living room carpet. I tried to explain that a hamster was a bit too big to get sucked up, but she wouldn't have it. She was demanding I pass on her complaint to the manufacturers, to get them to put a guard or something on the brush head, and all the time she kept breaking off to cry."

"The poor hamster," Daniel murmured. "Poor woman too."

"Poor woman my arse," I retorted. "She suddenly went quiet on me, and there was me going 'Madam? Madam?' wondering what the hell had happened. Then she says it's okay, she's just spotted the hamster climbing the curtains."

Daniel stared at me for a moment, then burst into laughter. God, he had a great laugh.

"Anyway, less about me. How are the rehearsals going?"

"Really well. We're doing two numbers on the stage in Trafalgar Square, and we've been working on one of them this week. Talk about risqué." Daniel fanned himself.

"Oh? Do tell."

Daniel leaned in as if he didn't want our fellow passengers to overhear. "I'm in a pair of tight black leather shorts and fishnet stockings, with a rainbow feather boa around my neck."

Okay, that conjured up a very specific image.

I couldn't resist. "Are you wearing the high-heeled boots for that one?"

Daniel stared at me, his eyes twinkling. "Oh. Got a thing for high heels, have we?" He bit his lip.

Now here's the weird part. High heels on a girl don't do a thing for me, but the thought of *Daniel* in them?

"I bet you look good in them. I think you look bloody amazing in make-up." Fuck. I hadn't meant to share that.

Daniel smiled. "Thank you. I always feel good when I put on a little paint." He leaned in close again. "And if I want to feel *really* good, I wear something lacy under my jeans."

OMG. Daniel was pushing buttons I hadn't even known I had.

Then he sat back, and I struggled to breathe evenly.

"Did you think about me this week?" Gone was the teasing tone, the sparkle in his eyes. It was obviously a serious question.

"Yeah, I did," I admitted. "A lot." More than I cared to share, because he'd think I was obsessed with him.

"And did you make any… decisions?" His gorgeous rich brown eyes were focused on mine, and it felt like he was holding his breath.

I wasn't going to let him die of oxygen starvation, now was I?

"Yes," I said in a firm voice. Then I smiled, although my heart was pounding. "Do you think we might go on another date?"

Fuck, the light in his face and eyes made my heartbeat quicken. "You mean that?"

I nodded. "A date. Not an experiment. I… I want to know you better."

Daniel's breathing hitched. "Then don't get off at Reading. Stay on the train. Come home with me."

"Tonight?" Okay, *that* got my heart beating even faster.

"Unless you have something urgent you need to do at home this evening?"

"No, I've got nothing planned." Only Friday night pizza, and I could give that a miss.

Daniel smiled. "Then come back to my place, and we'll have dinner. It might have to be takeaway, because I wasn't going shopping until tomorrow, but there's plenty of options nearby."

"Do we get to watch *How To Train Your Dragon* part two?" It sounded ridiculous even as I said it, but the thought of sitting on Daniel's sofa watching a film together made me warm inside.

He chuckled. "I think we can manage that." He tilted his head to one side. "And… do I get to kiss you again?"

I'd been thinking about Daniel's lips on mine every night since that kiss.

"Oh, I think we can manage that." How I sounded that nonchalant, I will never know.

Daniel drew in a deep breath. He said nothing, but then again he didn't need to—his smile said so much more than words ever could.

We sat in silence for the rest of the journey, but it didn't feel uncomfortable. I didn't want to talk anyway.

I was too busy imagining how our date was going to go. I was nervous, sure. Apprehensive even. But most of all, I was excited.

This was a new chapter, and I couldn't wait to see what was waiting for me on the next page.

"You sure you don't want a beer or a glass of wine?" Daniel asked as he cleared away the wrappings from our fish and chips.

"I'm sure. A coffee would be good though." Fish and chips had been an inspired choice. They smelled amazing and tasted even better. Once we'd arrived at the flat, I messaged Mick, telling him I wouldn't be around for Friday night pizza.

His reply was three question marks, followed by a winky emoji.

I sat on the sofa, reading the back of the DVD box. Hiccup looked older, and—dare I say it?—he was also cute.

"Hiccup grew up to be gorgeous, didn't he?" Daniel commented as he came back into the room. I blinked and dropped the plastic case onto the seat cushion beside me. Daniel grinned. "Oh, I see. I'm not the only one who thinks so."

"I am *not* lusting after an animated character, all right?"

Daniel held up his hands. "Whatever." He gestured to his clothing. "I hope you don't mind, but I needed to get out of my work clothes."

Mind? He was wearing a pair of denim shorts and a tank top that was perfect for the warm, almost summer evening. And he was beautiful. His legs were long and slim, with toned thighs and firm calves that looked perfect for a dancer. The sinuous way he moved as he walked across the room to join me was mesmerizing, and I couldn't tear my eyes off him.

"Are you cool enough?"

Lee Paul Tennant, stop that drooling this instant.

(Why does that voice sometimes have to sound like my *gran* of all people? Talk about a cock blocker.)

"I'm fine," I assured him. I'd rolled up my shirt sleeves and kicked off my shoes, but that was as far as I could go.

Daniel glanced at my black socks. "You *can* take them off, you know. I don't object to bare feet."

I peered lower, and sure enough, his feet were bare. And oh *fuck*, his toenails were a sparkly pink colour.

They looked *wonderful*.

Daniel flexed his toes, chuckling. "I love having my nails painted." He held up his hands and wiggled his fingers. "They match too." He peered at me. "Ever had your nails done?"

I was *so* glad I wasn't drinking at the time. "I can't see my cow of a supervisor liking *that*."

He grinned. "She can't see your toes though, can she?" His eyes gleamed. "Can I paint your toenails, Lee? Please?"

Fuck, he was serious.

Before I could get a word out—because for some reason my throat had seized and my mouth was as dry as a sandpit—Daniel tugged off my socks. He nodded approvingly. "I like a man who takes care of his feet." His gaze met mine. "Please, let me? I'll do a good job. I have toe spacers, base coat, topcoat, and any number of shades you can choose from." He grinned. "It'll be fun. Kind of a girls' night in."

I finally managed to breathe. I narrowed my gaze. "As long as we don't end up with you wanting to give me a makeover. I draw the line at make-up."

Daniel pouted, and it was an adorable look. "Aw."

I sighed. "I don't have a face for make-up. I'd look… silly."

To my surprise, Daniel sat beside me, his hand on my shoulder. "You wouldn't." He gently stroked my cheek. "And this is a beautiful face."

All I wanted in that instant was for him to lean in and kiss me, but he didn't. Instead, he stood and gave me a determined glance. "I'm going to fetch my stuff. And *then* I'm doing your toenails." And with that, he walked out of the room.

I tried to breathe evenly. In the space of a week, I'd gone from freaking out over him kissing me, to wanting to feel those lips on mine. Whether

I was ready for more than that, I didn't know, but I was taking things one step at a time.

Daniel walked back into the room, carrying a white plastic ice cream tub. He set it down on the sofa next to me, and removed pink curved foam and a couple of bottles of clear liquid. He pointed to the box. "Pick a colour."

I couldn't believe I was doing this. I peered into the box at the ten or so bottles, differing shades of pink, green, lilac, and—

"Oh wow." I picked up the bottle of purpley-blue polish that looked like a ton glitter had exploded inside it. It was so dark, so sparkly, with flakes that shimmered…

I fucking *loved* it.

"That's my favourite." Daniel grinned. "Okay, sit back. Now, is there anything you need before I start? Because you're going to be stuck there for a while."

If I was really going to do this… "Can I change my mind and have a glass of wine?"

He laughed. "I'll pour some for both of us." He went off to the kitchen.

I sagged against the cushions. I know I'd said it was a new chapter, but this wasn't *quite* what I'd envisaged. That didn't stop the pleasurable shudder of excitement that skittered down my spine.

Fifteen minutes later, I had a wine glass in my hand, while Daniel sat astride the end of the chaise, my feet between his thighs, propped up on a cushion with pink spacers stretching my toes apart, while he applied the first careful coat of polish on top of the base coat that had already dried. I stared at my feet, enthralled by the whole process.

"Will I need more than one coat?"

Daniel nodded absently, lost in concentration. He straightened, smiling triumphantly. "There. First coat on. What do you think?"

I thought my toes had never looked so pretty. "Now what?"

Daniel peered at my glass. "First off, I refill your glass while this coat hardens a little. Then I put on the second coat. When that's gone off, I add the clear topcoat to give your toes a bit of gloss, and hopefully prevent the colour from chipping off." He beamed. "A good job, if I say so myself."

I admired his handiwork. "You could do this for a living, if you ever get tired of working in a shop."

"I'll take that as a compliment." He got off the chaise and went in search of the wine bottle. When he returned, he poured us both some wine, then retook his position on the end of the chaise.

I couldn't help noticing his thighs, the muscles taut as he spread them, the way his shorts clung to them—and the obvious curve of his erection as it pressed against the zipper. I hastily swallowed a mouthful of wine, only it went down the wrong way, and I ended up spluttering.

Daniel arched his eyebrows, and for one heart-stopping moment, I was certain he knew where I'd been looking. "More haste, less speed?" he suggested, his lips twitching. Then he went back to his task, and I tried not to stare at the gorgeous expanse of flesh spread out before me.

Then it hit me. My heart was racing, my pulse was rapid, my breathing shallow—and my dick was stiff.

Since when did a guy's erection turn me on?

Chapter 8

"Lee?"

I forced myself back into the moment. Daniel was staring at me.

I gazed down at my feet and caught my breath. "That looks fantastic." The toe spacers were still in position. "Can I take those out now?" Anything not to think about my cock growing harder by the second.

"Not yet. I want to let the nails dry completely before I do that. They can smudge so easily." Daniel stood gracefully, and I tried not to look at his crotch. He put all the gear back into the plastic box before placing it on the floor. Then he joined me on the sofa after grabbing his wine glass. "So much for watching a film." He grinned. "This was much more fun."

I flexed my toes carefully. "It feels kind of wicked, going to work in a suit, and knowing this is how they look underneath." Little by little, my heartbeat was returning to normal.

He laughed. "Now perhaps you get why I like to wear less… conventional underwear when I go to work. It gives me a buzz, talking with customers and showing them clothes, looking the part of a sales assistant, while *underneath*…" His eyes shone. "Besides, it makes me feel sexy as fuck, and that can't be a bad thing, right?"

I couldn't answer. I was too busy picturing his dick nestled in lacy briefs.

"So, while I have you pinned here," he continued, "unable to move because heaven forbid you smudge that beautiful paint job I just did… maybe I should take advantage of the situation and kiss you." He didn't make a move though.

And there went my heart again, only this time I wasn't going to say *Whoa* after one kiss.

This time I wanted more.

I handed him my glass. "Want to put this somewhere?" I did my best to sound calm, but inside I was buzzing.

He took it, placing both glasses on the floor beside the box, out of harm's way. Then he shifted a little closer. "I've been thinking about doing this all week." His voice was soft, and the slight husky edge to it made me shiver.

"Me too." My breathing quickened as he cupped my neck, gazing into my eyes. I melted a little at that first brush of his lips against mine, as chaste as it had been a week ago.

"You can touch me, y'know," Daniel murmured before kissing me again, only now the kiss lingered, his fingers gentle as they wove through my hair, his touch almost as light as air.

I cupped the back of his head and held him there, our kiss morphing into something with a little more heat. When he touched my lips with his tongue, I opened for him after a second's hesitation, letting out a low noise of approval when he flicked my tongue with his. I shifted lower on the sofa, until I was almost lying down on the chaise, and he went with me, one leg hooked over mine as he locked us in an intimate embrace.

I couldn't get enough of him, his lips, his tongue, his hands on my neck and chest. I slid my fingers beneath his tank top, encountering smooth, warm flesh. My hands were on his waist, his back, moving restlessly as the kiss grew wetter, hotter, my tongue duelling with his. The subtle scrape of stubble against my face was new, and I didn't mind it one bit. He shifted to kneel on the chaise, one knee between my thighs, bending down to take my mouth over and over again, and I held onto him, one hand on his nape, the other on his back, connecting myself to him.

Daniel broke the kiss and knelt up. "Let me make it a little easier for you." With one swift move, he pulled his tank up and over his head, revealing his smooth torso, as lean and toned as I'd imagined. Silvery bars pierced his nipples, glinting in the light. I couldn't resist touching him, running my hands over his abs and taut belly. Then he bent over to kiss me again, and I sighed into it, needing his touch.

"More," I murmured. He stilled for a moment, his lips against mine, and then he was on top of me, his arms around me. I spread my legs, tugging him to lie between them.

"Your nails," he murmured, his eyes widening.

"Fuck my bloody nails," I groaned, before locking my arms around his neck and kissing him, my tongue exploring him as much as his explored me. Oh God, the smell of him… Whatever scent he wore invaded my nostrils, heady and warm, and I breathed him in. We couldn't stop kissing, both of us feeding the other noises that told me he was loving this as much as I was.

When he kissed my neck, I shivered and gave him room, shuddering as he flicked my earlobe with his tongue before tugging gently on it. He was in constant motion like a wave on the shore, slow and sensual, and I relished the feel of his body against mine. His hard body.

Oh *fuck*. Daniel was hard.

He rolled his hips, and there it was again, his hard-on against my dick. No mistaking it. A slow sexy rotation dragged his shaft over mine, my heart hammered, and I tensed.

Daniel stilled instantly. He looked into my eyes, his lips parted, his breathing staccato. "And that's my cue to stop."

I swallowed. I wasn't about to argue.

Daniel rose to his knees on the chaise and

reached for his tank top that he'd tossed aside. He pulled it over his head. "I'm sorry."

I ignored my quickened heartbeat and gaped at him. "For what? Kissing me? Because trust me, I wanted that as much as you did. And I'm not as new to this as I was last week. I… I've been doing some research."

Daniel blinked and sat back on his haunches. "Research?"

I nodded, my chin high. "I watched all of Queer as Folk."

It was Daniel's turn to gape. "Tell me you mean the UK original. Because it would have taken you *days* to watch the US version."

I rolled my eyes. "Yes, the UK one." I was calmer, my heart returning to its natural rhythm.

Daniel grinned. "I'm impressed." He held out a hand to me and helped me to sit upright. He cupped my face in his hands and leaned in to kiss me lightly on the lips. He sighed as he released me. "Okay… I know I said last week that I couldn't wait to see what you're like in bed, but that was before."

"Before what?"

He gave me a meaningful stare. "Before I knew what the state of play was. So… what I'm saying now is… I want to go slower. I had every *intention* of going slower—until we started kissing."

Okay, that made me feel pretty pleased with

myself. I buffed my fingernails on my shirt. "What can I say? It's a gift."

Daniel raised his eyes heavenward.

Except I couldn't be flippant, not when he'd made me feel so amazing. I looped my arms around his neck. "I know what you mean about the kissing. What is it about you that makes me feel like I'm a teenager all over again, making out for the first time?" Because that was *exactly* how it had felt.

He grinned. "What can I say? It's a gift." I hit him on the arm, and he gave me a mock glare. "Ow."

"So what now?" I didn't mind taking things slow. I might have been ready to make out on the sofa with him, but judging by my reaction to his hard-on, that was as far as my body was prepared to go right then.

After another week of research, who knows how I'd feel?

Daniel got up off the chaise and sat beside me. "What are you doing tomorrow night?"

I arched my eyebrows. "Do you have something in mind?"

He nodded. "A date. A night that isn't dinner at my place."

I snorted. "As long as you're not thinking of dinner at *my* place."

His eyes glittered. "Actually, I was thinking of… dancing."

"Where?"

"London. Soho. A gay bar called Freedom, where they serve great cocktails, but downstairs there's this fantastic dance floor."

"A gay bar?" Okay, my heart was doing its little dance again.

Daniel chuckled. "Have you ever *been* to a gay bar?"

I huffed. "No, but there are *lots* of places I haven't been to."

"Then we're going to Freedom. You might even find yourself hobnobbing with celebs."

"Why? Who goes to this place?"

"Some of the dancers and their partners from Strictly." That great smile was back. "If *they* can enjoy a night in the company of gay guys, I'm sure *you* can. Besides, it's not all guys—women go there too." He cocked his head to one side. "So it's a date? I'll meet you at the statue of Eros at Piccadilly. It'll be busy there, so I'll make sure you won't be able to miss me." Daniel's eyes sparkled. "I'll be wearing my rainbow feather boa and fishnet stockings."

Okay, he had me going for about two seconds before I realized he was pulling my leg. That earned him another playful whack on the arm. Then I remembered I owed him an answer. "It's a date then." Even if the thought set off this quivery feeling in the pit of my stomach.

He beamed, and the sight eased my heart

palpitations.

(Okay, it wasn't *that* bad, but you get the idea, right?)

Daniel picked up my wine glass and handed it to me. "You don't *have* to go home tonight," he murmured. "I do have a spare bedroom, remember."

And there went my heart again.

I had to be honest with him. "If I'm going to stay, I'd like to be prepared for it. You know, with a toothbrush, a change of clothes, stuff like that…"

He nodded. "Yeah. I understand." His voice was quiet.

"No, you *don't*." I placed my hand on his knee. "Because if I ever decide to spend a night here…" Fuck, my heart… "I don't want to be sleeping in your spare bed, all right?" There, I'd said it.

Daniel studied me for a moment. "'If I ever' sounds a bit vague, like… it might not happen."

Just say it. You know you want to.

I took a deep breath. "When I stay the night, it'll be in your bed. All right?"

His breathing hitched, and I had the feeling I'd said the right thing. "All right. I'll look forward to that."

It sounded like an agreement, and what surprised the hell out of me was that I didn't mind that at all. There was no time frame attached to it, no deadline, just the understanding that it would happen one day.

Or should that be night?

Whatever. There was a lightness in my chest, my pulse was rapid, and adrenaline was flooding through me at the thought of being in his bed.

Don't think about this now. Later.

I finished my wine. "I think I'd better go." I got to my feet, and he joined me. Before I could utter another word, he kissed me, taking his time.

I could get used to this.

Then I became aware of an ache in my toe joints. One that hadn't been there before.

"Daniel?" I murmured against his lips between kisses.

"Mm?"

"Can I take the toe spacers out now, please?"

He laughed, and I could feel the vibrations through his body. "Sure. Let me do it." He knelt at my feet and carefully removed the pink foam pieces. "How does that look?"

I glanced down, and all I saw was Daniel on his knees in front of me, his face within inches of my crotch. He tilted his head to gaze up at me, and when he licked his lower lip, a delightful shiver ran through me. "Looks… great," I muttered.

Daniel rose to his feet, moving gracefully, until he was looking me in the eye. "I was talking about your toes," he murmured, his lips twitching.

I blinked. "My toes?" I glanced down at them and grinned. "Hey, look at that. Not one smudge."

Daniel laughed. "Do you know how funny that was? 'Fuck my bloody nails,'" he mimicked.

Now that he mentioned it…

Both of us laughed, until Daniel stopped me with another kiss. A deep, sparkly-purpley-blue, toe-curling kiss. Instinctively I cupped the back of his head, returning the kiss with all of me, including soft moans. I had one hand on his back, my fingers once again seeking flesh beneath his tank top.

(Okay, I was itching to touch his nipples. I'd heard piercings make them extra-sensitive, and I wanted to see if that was true.)

"Fuck, you're addictive," I murmured against his lips.

Daniel pulled back and laughed again. "Says you. I can't get enough of you."

"You can have more tomorrow night." Then I thought about it. "Will it be okay to kiss you at this bar?"

Daniel bit his lip. "I think you might be able to get away with it." With a sigh, he pushed me away. "You need to go. I only have so much willpower, you know." He grabbed my jacket from the back of the dining chair and held it for me while I put it on. Then he handed me my bag. "Just so you know… I can't wait to see you again," he said in a low voice.

"Ditto." One word, but I meant it with my whole heart.

He walked me downstairs to the front door, and before I stepped out into the night air, Daniel took me in his arms, and we exchanged one last lingering kiss.

"See you tomorrow."

I nodded. "I'll look out for the feather boa."

Daniel was laughing as he closed the door.

I walked up the street toward the station, lighter and happier than I'd ever felt before. I was on autopilot, my mind still in his living room, on his sofa, kissing…

Okay. Kissing a guy. It wasn't all *that* different from kissing a girl—and yet it was. I know, I know. That makes no sense. There were subtle differences, of course—stubble, for one thing. And when he let himself go, there was more… steel in his kiss, I suppose. I know *I* didn't hold back either.

I couldn't wait to kiss him again.

Half an hour later, I was back in the house. Judging by the sounds coming from the lounge, they were watching a horror film. I'd know Justin's squeals anywhere.

I tiptoed past the room, intending to go up to my room, but the door opened as I reached the stairs.

“Was it a good night?” It was Mick.

I paused and turned, smiling. I don’t think I’d stopped smiling since I left Daniel’s flat. “Yeah. I had a great time.”

Mick stared at me, smirking. “So I see.”

I frowned. “What do you mean?”

He chuckled, before taking my arm and tugging me toward the mirror on the wall. Mick turned me to face it and stood behind me. “Notice anything?” He was still smirking.

Oh my God. The light in the hall wasn’t *that* bright, but I could still see my lips were redder than usual and a little swollen. Plus, there was reddening of the skin around my chin and mouth.

Mick leaned in and whispered, “Yeah, you had a *very* good time, didn’t you?”

I had to laugh. “That’s because he’s a very good kisser,” I whispered back. I stared at my reflection, my fingers gently touching my lips.

I looked well and truly kissed.

I headed for the stairs once more, and Mick followed me to the foot of them. “Tell him to shave first next time. Besides, you don’t want a rash anywhere… delicate.”

Okay, it took a moment for his meaning to sink in. I gaped at him. “We didn’t… we weren’t… I haven’t…”

Mick laughed quietly. “Okay, okay, I believe you. Think of it as advice for the future.” He inclined his head toward the lounge. “I’d better get back in there. Justin might need someone to hold his hand in the scary bits." Right on cue, Justin's loud howl of fright filled the air. Mick shook his head. "Too late."

I chuckled and went to climb the stairs.

"Lee?"

I stopped again. "Yeah?"

Mick was still standing at the foot of the stairs. "A word of warning, from someone who's been in your shoes." He gestured to my lips. "Just so you know? It'll be more noticeable tomorrow."

I stared at him, aghast. "Aw crap."

Mick nodded. "Be ready, because you *know* this lot. They're not going to keep quiet, not when they have the chance to take the piss." Then he went back into the room.

I climbed the stairs, my fingers carefully touching my lips. *This is a first.* But as I closed my bedroom door behind me, I realized there were more firsts to come.

I don't know if I was excited or scared.

Chapter 9

June 16, 2018

You can't beat a Saturday morning lie-in.

No work to drag myself out of bed for. A quiet house, because apart from Moz and Niall who are already at work, the others aren't about yet. The distant drone of traffic, because the rest of the world is up-and-at-'em, even if I'm not. And the best thing about a lie-in?

I have all the time in the world for a really good wank.

That morning, I had more than usual stored in my wank bank. Sometimes it was porn, but mostly I relied on fantasies, playing them out in my head as I lay there, stroking my shaft with a slick palm, the duvet kicked off and my feet planted on the mattress.

This particular wank was all about Daniel.

I closed my eyes, my dick held loosely as I tugged gently on it, my legs spread with one foot flat to the bed. He was there, kneeling at my feet in his living room, gazing up at me with those beautiful brown eyes, and his mouth mere inches from my crotch. I slowed my stroke, pulling softly on my balls with my free hand, picturing his glossy lips.

Which he was licking.

The slick sound of my dick only served to heighten my arousal. Fantasy Daniel reached for the button on my pants while he smiled at me. “Can I?”

What horny male in his right mind was going to say no to a warm, wet mouth on his cock?

I nodded, my hand working my shaft a little faster, only now I was tweaking my nipple, slowly rubbing over it with my thumb. Daniel lowered the zipper, reached into my suddenly tight-as-fuck briefs, and freed my dick. I had no time to say a word before he flicked the head with his tongue, then proceeded to take it carefully into his mouth.

I screwed my eyes tight shut, as if opening them would dispel the sight of Daniel sucking my cock like he *really* needed it. I placed my hands on his head and urged him to take it deeper, my hips rocking up off the bed as I fucked his gorgeous mouth, those soft lips tight around my shaft.

I needed more.

I opened my eyes, rolled onto my belly and stuffed a pillow under me. Then I propped myself up and started humping it, driving my dick into its softness, fucking it like I wanted to fuck Daniel’s mouth, hearing him moan around it as I got closer, closer…

With a stifled cry I shot into the pillow, my

body shaking, my arms trembling. In my head, Daniel's lips were covered with my spunk, and he cleaned them with a leisurely tongue, making me shiver.

"You taste delicious." His eyes sparkled.

I grabbed my dick and brushed the head against his lower lip, his tongue snaking out to lick it tantalizingly slowly, before—

My phone burst into life with a call.

Fuck. Fuck. Fuck.

I reached for it, cursing myself for forgetting to put it on mute the night before. When I saw the caller, I groaned. *Mum.*

(Yes, I know I've only got one mum. Yes, of course I love her. But try to think how *you'd* feel if you'd just come, you hadn't cleaned up yet, and your mum wanted to talk to you.)

I clicked on answer and switched to speaker phone while I disrobed the pillow and wiped myself clean with its now soiled cotton covering. "Morning, Mum."

"Good morning. I haven't disturbed you, have I?"

"No, you're fine." It could've been worse, right? She could've called me mid-hump.

"I'm just ringing to remind you about tomorrow, that's all."

Tomorrow? My mind was a complete blank. All I could think of was my date later with Daniel.

She sighed. "Yeah. That silence is very

telling. Sunday lunch, remember? Your sister's coming too, and Ben."

Mum did a once-a-month Sunday lunch for the family, which was usually my parents, my sister Rachel and her husband Ben, and me. Three hours of sitting around, eating the standard fare of roast chicken, roast potatoes, peas and carrots, covered with Mum's version of gravy, (No gravy granules in *that* house, thank you very much—Dad would have a fit.) and trying to avoid conversations that always began with 'So are you seeing anyone?'

Torture.

"I hadn't forgotten," I said, lying through my teeth. Well, come *on*. I'd had a lot on my mind the last week, right? "Same time as usual?" Which meant be there by midday or else.

"Yes."

"Can I bring a bottle of wine?" Anything to make the time more pleasurable and pass quicker. So maybe *two* bottles of wine would be better in that case.

"Yes, but don't expect your dad to have any of it."

I stifled my snort. Dad was a hardened bitter drinker. Wine was for *other people*.

"And your sister says she's got some news."

I fervently hoped Ben hadn't got a new job and they were leaving the area. They lived about three streets away from our parents, which was great for me. Mum was always popping round to see Rach on some pretext or other, but Rach didn't seem to mind. She and Mum were pretty tight.

But if they *moved…*

Nope. I wasn't going to think about it. I wasn't even going to *talk* about it. "I'll be there," I said in a bright voice. "See you then." And I disconnected in a hurry. I'd deal with whatever Rachel's news was when I saw her. Right then I was starving.

I dragged on a pair of sweats, went over to the door and peered out onto the landing. I couldn't hear water running in the bathroom, so I grabbed a towel and legged it down the stairs to the first floor to the house's one and only bathroom.

You learn to be quick when there's five of you and only one shower.

A glance in the mirror revealed Mick's prediction to have been accurate. My lips were still a little swollen but the rash on my chin and cheeks was more pronounced. My first thought was not of my housemates' reactions, but of my approaching date.

I can't go out like this! Well, not without a paper bag over my head.

By the time I walked into the kitchen in search of something for breakfast, Mick had made a pot of tea, and Niall was busy with the toaster. He turned toward me as he was about to place a slice of bread in the slot and froze. "Oh… oh my." His gaze flickered toward Mick.

I waved my hand. "You're okay. He knows."

Niall nodded. He bit his lip. "I guess I don't have to ask if things are going well, do I?"

Mick snorted, then hurriedly cleared his throat. "Tea?" he asked, pointing to the pot.

"Sure." I gestured to my face. "I need to come up with a plan though. I've got a date tonight."

Mick's eyes gleamed with approval. "Another date? Things *are* going well. Where to? Anywhere nice?"

"Dancing in a gay bar in Soho." Then it hit me. "What am I going to wear?"

Niall chuckled. "What you *usually* wear."

"But it's a *gay* bar."

Mick laughed. "And?" He rolled his eyes and pointed to the table. "Sit. When you've had some tea and toast, we'll come upstairs with you and we'll go through your wardrobe. You must have *something* that'll make you look fantastic." He poured out a mug of tea and handed it to me. "Get that how you like it, and Niall will make the toast. Then we'll sit *calmly* and eat breakfast."

I couldn't resist. "Yes, *Dad*." Both of them laughed. "But I still need to think about disguising this." I pointed to my lips and chin.

"There's always make-up," Niall suggested,

his eyes sparkling.

I was about to glare at him when an idea occurred. I pulled my phone from my pocket and texted Daniel.

You awake?

Seconds later my phone rang. “This is a recording. Daniel is still in bed, but if you leave a message, he’ll be sure to—”

“Ha ha, very funny. This is serious.”

“Why, what’s wrong?” Daniel’s voice changed instantly, and I couldn’t miss the concerned note.

“What’s wrong is my face is a mess, *that’s* what’s wrong,” I retorted. “And it’s all your fault.”

“Next time, shave before you snog him,” Mick yelled, and I did manage a glare that time.

“That’s Mick, one of my housemates, and if he does that again, he’ll be an *ex*-housemate.”

Daniel laughed. “Oh dear. Well, at least I know what the problem is.” He softened his voice. “Is it really bad?”

“Bad enough that I am *not* walking into Freedom looking like this.”

“Oh, I don’t know. If you’re with me, I’m going to get a *lot* of jealous glances.”

I shook my head. “How do you do that? I should be mad at you, but instead, you’re making me feel good.”

“I’m glad.” That soft voice was stirring something inside me.

"But there's a way you can make me feel even better."

"Yeah?"

"Bring your make-up with you tonight. You could fix this, couldn't you?" I *hoped.*

Daniel didn't laugh. "I'll bring foundation and face powder."

I heaved a sigh of relief.

"I might also bring some eye make-up and lipstick," he added.

I stiffened. "Why?"

"Oh, no reason." Daniel replied in a light tone that didn't fool me for a second. "We'll meet as planned, and then I'll take you somewhere to apply the foundation before we go on to Freedom. How's that?"

"Perfect." I breathed a little easier.

"Then I'll see you at Eros, as arranged. Are your lips sore?" That note of concern was back.

"No, just a little bruised-looking, to add to the stubble rash."

"I'm not in the least bit sorry." Daniel's voice was husky. "I have no regrets."

I swallowed, aware of the warmth spreading through my body. "Me neither." I disconnected the call. Then I realized the room was silent.

Mick and Niall were staring at me.

I pointed to the toaster. "Get toasting! We've got things to do!" I went to the fridge to get the milk, my pulse quickening.

He is not *getting me to wear more make-up than I need to.*

#LoveWins
love is love

I scanned the crowds around the statue, searching for Daniel. He'd been right about the number of people. I stood there for about ten minutes, and there was no sign of him. I knew he was coming—there'd been no message to call it off—but that didn't stop my stomach from churning.

This was new.

This was a real date

Not that they hadn't been dates before, but being out in public with him, dancing with him… My mouth was dry, and I wished I'd brought a bottle of water with me. Butterflies were already dancing in my stomach, by the feel of it.

"Hello there."

I gave a start and swung around to face him. "Christ, you made me jump."

Daniel chuckled. "Sorry." He looked as gorgeous as every other time we'd met, in tight black jeans, his black Skechers, and a horizontal striped top that clung to his body. He carried a lightweight black jacket in one hand, and the strap of his bag was slung across his chest. A touch of purple accentuated the corners of his eyes, and the smudge of eye liner around them was breath-taking.

He grinned. "Will I do?"

I took a deep breath. "You are as stunning as always."

Daniel's lips parted, and he caught his breath. "Thank you." He looked me up and down before breaking into a beautiful smile. "Oh really, thank you." He said it with such sincerity that my worries about my clothing dissipated. Niall had insisted on me wearing jeans, but Mick had picked out a top I'd rarely worn, made from a soft white fabric that draped beautifully, with a scoop neckline low enough to reveal a lot of my chest.

Daniel traced my breastbone with gentle fingers. "I like this. I also like that you're as bare here as I am."

"I once grew three hairs on my chest. It was all I could manage." I sighed dramatically. "They withered away from embarrassment." It felt strange to have him touch me so intimately in the middle of a crowded street corner, but it also set my heart beating faster.

He laughed, before touching my lips with such care that I almost melted. "Poor you. Can I kiss them better?"

We're in public.

We're in public.

"Yes," I whispered, and he closed the gap between us, kissing me lightly on the lips, a chaste, tender kiss.

A *just right* kiss.

(Get me. I'm beginning to sound like Goldilocks.)

Then he pulled back. "Now let's fix this," he said, his fingertips gentle on my chin. He pointed in the direction of the Tube station. "The toilets in there will do. The light will be awful, but at least I'll see everything. Plus, the lighting in Freedom won't be as harsh."

I followed him into the station and into the nearest Gents toilet. Once inside, we went over to the sinks, and Daniel rummaged in his bag, removing a couple of bottles and a compact.

"I wasn't sure which would be closer to your shade. Your skin tone is a little warmer than mine, but not that dissimilar." He opened both and put a dab from each onto my chin.

A guy in a suit came into the toilets, took one look at us, and promptly turned around and walked out.

Daniel huffed. "What's *his* problem? You'd think he'd never seen two guys putting on make-up before." His eyes twinkled. Then he peered closer. "This one, I think." He put the other bottle back in his bag, then removed a small square flat sponge, onto which he poured a little foundation. He applied it carefully, blending it until he was happy with the result. Finally, he applied another sponge, this one covered with face powder, pressing it firmly against my skin, then blending again.

"Are you done?" I asked, trying to turn and see.

"Don't be so impatient. I'm going to put a little over your whole face, so it looks uniform."

"Everywhere?" I wasn't sure I was ready for a face full of make-up.

"Trust me," he said as he pressed the powder under my eyes, on my cheekbones and my forehead, and along my jawline. He straightened, then turned me toward the mirror above the sink. "Well? Is that better?"

Better? It was freaking *fantastic*.

"I love it."

Daniel let out an audible sigh of relief.

Then I narrowed my gaze. "Is there *more* make-up in that bag?"

"There is," he said with a touch of hesitation. "But to be honest, now that I see you like this? You don't need it." He bit his lip. "Except… I'd love to put just a smidge of lip gloss on you. Or maybe… lipstick?" He reached into his bag and held up a small clear tube of pink liquid and a lipstick in a black case.

"It's pink."

Daniel chuckled. "How observant. So is the lipstick. And they will look *amazing* on you. Try it, please? For me?"

As if I could refuse him. "Okay," I said, my heartbeat quickening again.

Daniel rolled up the lipstick and applied it carefully, before blotting it with a piece of tissue. "This is not what *I* do when I'm putting on lipstick and gloss, but we haven't got time for that." He applied a second coat and blotted it again, before adding the lip gloss. "*Now* what do you think?"

I stared at my reflection. It wasn't me staring back—it was someone *far* more good-looking. My skin appeared flawless. My lips looked… luscious. There was no other word for them.

Daniel stood behind me. "I think you look fabulous," he said quietly. "And I also think every guy in Freedom is going to want to scratch my eyes out, because *I'll* be the one dancing with you." He put away the make-up, then met my gaze in the mirror. "Ready?"

I took a deep breath. "Ready."

For what, I had no idea.

Chapter 10

"You weren't kidding when you said it would be busy," I commented as we stepped through the doors into Freedom. The place was *heaving*. I couldn't see the bar because of the sheer number of people gathered there. Music played, something with a heavy bass that pulsed through the floor. There were booths around the outside of the space, all of them occupied.

Daniel leaned in to speak above the music, as we were standing right next to the DJ. "It's always like this. You should see it at Pride. It's worse." Then he let out a happy cry. "Oh wow."

I followed the direction of his glance to see a couple seated in one of the booths. The woman was waving frantically at him. "I take it they're friends of yours?"

"Really good friends," Daniel replied warmly. "Come and meet them." He led me over to the booth, where a padded bench curved around three quarters of a circular table. The couple stood and came out from behind it to greet Daniel with exuberant hugs. Daniel gestured to me. "This is Lee." He pointed to the man, who was tall with maybe the darkest shade of black skin I'd ever seen. "This is Troy. We go way back."

Troy extended a hand to me. "Pleased to meet you, Lee." He gripped my hand in a firm shake.

I couldn't shake the feeling I'd seen him before. "Have we met?" He was very handsome, with a strong, clean jawline and wide shoulders.

Daniel chuckled. "You might have seen him in magazines. Troy's a model."

I gaped. "That's it. You've been in magazines modelling clothes."

Troy held up both hands. "Please, no autographs." I laughed. He gestured to the woman beside him, who was almost as short as he was tall, petite with short blond hair. "This is my girlfriend, Caroline."

She took my hand. "I was hoping you'd be here tonight." Both Troy and Daniel gave her a hard stare, but she dismissed them with a wave. "I think you two should go and get the drinks in." She glanced toward the bar. "You might be a while."

Daniel met my gaze. "I won't be long."

It warmed me that he was looking out for me, but I was a big boy. I could take care of myself. And glancing at the occupants of the bar, I felt right at home. I'm not sure what I'd expected to see, but this crowd looked like pretty much like every other crowd I'd ever seen out for a Saturday night dancing session. "I'll be fine." I grinned. "I'd like a cocktail please. You can choose. I'm not fussy."

Daniel's eyes gleamed. "Do you like passion fruit?" When I nodded, he sighed happily. "Then I know exactly what to get you." He tugged Troy's arm. "Come on." Then he glanced at Caroline. "If we're not back in half an hour, send help." She chuckled. Daniel narrowed his gaze. "And behave."

"Me?" Caroline's eyes were wide in an expression of innocence.

Daniel rolled his eyes before walking away from the table with Troy. As soon as they were gone, Caroline patted the seat next to her. "Sit. I have so many questions."

Puzzled, I slid into the booth. Something clicked into place. "You were hoping *I'd* be here tonight?" She'd looked at me as she said it.

Caroline nodded. "I hoped he'd bring you. I have to say, I've been dying to meet you."

I blinked. "Me?"

She laughed. "Sweetheart, Daniel has done nothing but talk about you every night for the past week."

Okay, I blinked again. "Me?"

Caroline leaned against the padded back of the seat. "Last Friday night, he called me, so excited, like I haven't heard him in a long while. He said he'd met a really cute guy on the train, they'd talked, and he'd asked him out. What excited him was that he'd seen the guy before a few times, and had been dying to say something, but the right moment had never arisen."

Okay. That stopped me dead in my tracks. "He'd been wanting to talk to me *before* that day?"

She nodded. "He couldn't believe it when you started talking to him first. Poor love, he was so nervous. He said he had to ask you out, because he didn't know if he'd ever get the chance again."

I couldn't think of Daniel as nervous. He always seemed so self-assured.

"Then when you said yes, his nerves really kicked in." Caroline studied me. "That's when I knew."

"Knew what?"

She smiled. "That you were important to him. Daniel doesn't get into such a mess over a guy. So I knew you were different."

"But… he didn't know anything about me." That was what I couldn't get past. How could I have made such an impression so fast?

"He called me Saturday night, and I knew right away something was wrong."

I took a breath. "I told him I wasn't gay. And… let's just say we ran before we could walk."

She nodded again. "He told me all about it."

"You two must be close."

Caroline's smile reached her eyes. "Yeah. We were at school together. In fact, Daniel was the one who introduced me to Troy." She chuckled. "I liked the way you described yourself. 'Mostly straight with a dash of gayness.'"

I stared at her. "He really did tell you everything." Well, I hoped not *every*thing.

Caroline laced her hands on the table. "I know last week was hard on him. He was waiting to hear what you'd decided, and it was driving him crazy."

"It was a strange week for me too," I muttered. When she gave me a quizzical glance, I sighed. "Look at it from my perspective. I'd never been attracted to guys before. Then suddenly a guy asks me out on a date, and I said yes. I wasn't sure why."

"Did you reach any conclusions?"

I smiled. "Yeah. It had to be something about Daniel. I'd met the only man to push my buttons."

A couple of guys walked past our table and waved at Caroline, who waved back. One of them caught me looking and smiled. I couldn't help myself. I smiled back. He stopped and came back to us.

"Well, hello there." He had a deep, rough voice that I really liked. He wore a sexy black leather gilet that left his muscular arms bare and revealed a mat of dense chest hair.

"Hi." I tried not to stare at his chest and arms.

(Okay, so I was trying not to drool. Happy

now?)

"Are you here with Caro?" he asked. "And will you be around when the dance floor opens later?" His eyes sparkled. "Because if you are, I'll be sure to find you."

Okay, who turned the heat up in there?

Before I could reply, Caroline dove in. "No, he's not here with me, he's with Daniel, yes, he probably will be dancing, and no, Max, you and Carl are *not* going to make him the filling for your sandwich. It's his first time here, and he doesn't play like that."

Max pulled a face. "Pity." His eyes met mine. "See you on the dance floor." He gave me a sexy grin, revealing gleaming white teeth, before walking off to join his partner.

I watched him go, unable to miss that tight arse encased in even tighter denim. *Damn. You could bounce a pound coin off that thing.*

Caroline cleared her throat, and I blinked. She was smirking. "So it's just Daniel, hmm? Never been attracted to guys before, hmm?"

I can admit when I'm wrong.

I coughed. "Okay. Maybe 'mostly straight' isn't quite right."

Her eyes gleamed. "You don't say." Then she laughed. "Contrary to popular belief, there's nothing wrong with being bi. I should know." She tugged her small black bag into view, and tapped a badge attached to the strap. It had three stripes in pink, purple and blue.

"What is that?" I didn't recognize it.

"*That* is the bisexual pride flag." She arched her eyebrows. "We *have* heard of bisexuality, have we?"

It was like talking to Daniel about Pride, all over again.

I rolled my eyes. "Yes, *we* have." Not that I knew anyone who was bi. Then I reasoned that might not be the case. For all I knew, I could be *surrounded* by lesbian, gay, bi and trans people at work. But like Mick said, if they were, it was no one's business but theirs.

Then I thought about her statement. "What do you mean, contrary to popular belief? And am I bi then?"

She arched her eyebrows again. "Are you in some doubt about it?"

"Well, I wasn't sure. I mean, it's not exactly fifty-fifty. I've dated women up till now."

Caroline laughed. "It's a bit more fluid than that. You can be attracted more to girls than guys, or the other way around."

"Then it's okay to prefer one over the other?" I had to admit, this was even more new territory for me to explore.

"Of course. Just be prepared, okay? It's not going to be all plain sailing." Her face tightened a little.

Okay, now she had me worried. "What do

you mean?"

She sighed. "Look, attitudes have changed a lot in the last few years, yeah? People are more open to others being gay or lesbian. But that openness doesn't extend to people who are bi, I'm sad to say."

"Why not?" And how come I wasn't aware of this? Then I reconsidered. I was someone who never saw the point of going to Pride, remember? Why the hell would I be bothered to learn about people who were LGBT?

The realization made my face tingle and my throat tighten.

Caroline huffed. "Where do I start with the ignorant assumptions people make? Let's see." She counted off on her fingers. "Bis are promiscuous. They're not monogamous. If you're bi, that means you indulge in threesomes and orgies."

I snorted. "Sounds like some people are jealous, if you ask me."

She laughed. "You know, I'd never thought of it from that angle. But seriously, people see being bi as a 'phase,'" she air-quoted. "Bis can't make up their minds, so it's an excuse to fuck anything that moves. And there's this phrase I hate, one that Troy hears a lot. 'Bi now, gay later.'" Caroline shuddered. "He's dated guys in the past, I've dated girls. Just because I live with a guy doesn't make me het. I'm still attracted to women. But I don't play the field and neither does he."

That raised a worry in my mind. “Do you think Daniel is scared I’ll find someone else—a girl—and decide I’m straight after all? That he’s just a ‘phase’?”

She regarded me frankly. “What do *you* think you are?”

I fell silent, my mind going over what she’d said. I didn’t have to think for long. “I’m bi,” I said at last. Mick could say what he liked about labels. I didn’t have a problem with that particular one. So what if I’d only ever dated girls up till now?

Now there was Daniel.

Caroline leaned in and kissed my cheek. “Welcome to the club, sweetheart.”

“Are we interrupting something?” Daniel stood at the table, holding two cocktail glasses filled to the brim with an orange-coloured liquid. When he placed them on the table, I peered into the glass. Half a passion fruit was floating in it, and it was on fire.

“That is really cool. What is it?”

Daniel grinned. “A porn star martini. Try it.”

I glared. “Do you *want* me to burn my eyebrows off?”

“I think they expect you to blow it out first,” Troy said with a twinkle in his eye. He sat beside Caroline, placing a tall glass in front of her. “Your mojito, babe.”

Daniel slid into the booth beside me. “I

think a toast is in order."

"Can I make it?" I said on impulse.

He smiled. "Sure."

I raised my glass. "To new friends." All three of them smiled at that and echoed my toast. I blew on mine, extinguishing the flame before I took a sip. "Ooh, this is good." I drank a little more, my mind still working over everything Caroline had said. It seemed like I'd chosen a difficult path for myself. I knew one thing for certain: I wasn't going to share my realizations with anyone in my family until I had cause to do so. And that would be in only one circumstance—if I took a boyfriend to meet them. So far, Daniel was a date. Time would tell if he was going to be more than that.

The thought of 'more than that' made me shiver with anticipation.

The ceiling was covered with glittering disco balls, laser lights flickering over them and the dancers below, and above the bar were chandeliers.

As dance floors went, this was great. Every inch of the floor was covered with bodies moving to the music, in pairs or singly, in groups or swinging around the dance poles located here and there. The music was varied: so far, I'd danced my feet off to Lady Gaga's *Stupid Love*, Jax Jones' *This Is Real*, Jonas Blue's *Mistakes*, and Celeste's *Stop This Flame*. The four of us had danced together, and I had to admit, Daniel was a wonderful mover. I could've spent all night just *watching* him. And as for me, I didn't care who saw me, I was having such a good time. I lost myself in the music and threw my heart, body and soul into my dancing, loving every minute of it. It had been a while since I'd gone out dancing, and I was making up for lost time.

Once we came down to the dance floor, however, it felt less like a date and more like a Saturday night dancing. Not that I minded—I was having a great time. (Besides, it's a little difficult to be alone with someone in the middle of a packed floor, right?)

I took a breather around 1.00 a.m., standing by the bar with Caroline while Troy and Daniel stayed on the dance floor. We watched them, and I couldn't help noticing the admiring glances they received from some of the dancers around them, of both sexes.

"Why aren't you dancing?" Caroline said loudly above the music.

"I'm pacing myself," I said with a grin. I intended being there until they closed. Then it would be a case of finding somewhere for breakfast, before catching the first train home, which wasn't until seven in the morning. It was only then I realized I had no idea what Daniel was doing afterward.

Breakfasting with me, I hope. At least I'd get him alone. He *definitely* wasn't alone right then: the pack of admirers was growing.

Part of me didn't like that at all, which surprised me. I wasn't one to get jealous.

"Can I ask you something?" Caroline said into my ear.

"You can ask," I joked, my gaze still fixed on Daniel.

"Are you sure there was *nothing* to indicate you might like guys before you met Daniel? Not that I'm doubting you, but…"

I glanced at her. She was grinning. I deliberated for a moment. "If I tell you something, you have to promise not to breathe a word. *Especially* to Daniel."

"*Oh*. This sounds intriguing." She put her hand to her heart. "Okay, I promise."

"Well…" I couldn't believe I was going to share this. "When I was a teenager, I used to borrow my mum's catalogue, take it up to my room… and go through it, looking at the photos."

Her lips twitched. "*Which* photos?"

I sighed. "The underwear section. I used to look at the lingerie, trying to spot nipples or… anything else. And… I'd look at the men's briefs too." My cheeks grew hot.

Caroline put her arm around my shoulder and pulled me in for a hug. "I don't think you were the only one, sweetheart." She released me. "Was that it then? Because that's not shocking. We've all been there."

"No, that wasn't it." I took the plunge. "Whenever I watched porn—het porn, I'm talking about—I always preferred the guys to the girls."

Caroline laughed. "Me too. I can't stand lesbian porn. I prefer guys."

"Really?"

She nodded. "The girls are always so… loud. I never make *that* much noise, and I *never* say things like that when I'm… you get the picture."

"Exactly! Whereas the guys were all lean and quiet, and just got down to the business in hand. And whenever they showed a couple from behind, I was usually looking at his arse rather than anything else." Firm cheeks hollowing as he thrust deep, the rhythmic motion of those round globes, his thighs, the muscles straining…

Fuck. I was deluding myself, wasn't I? Talk about being in denial.

Caroline stared at me. "And you thought you were totally straight." She was trying not to laugh, I could tell. And that was all I needed to see the funny side of it.

I burst out laughing. "Okay, okay." At least

I could finally be honest with myself. All it had taken was meeting Daniel. I glanced across to where he was dancing and I froze, my jaw clenched and my stomach tensing.

Caroline followed my gaze. "Bloody Max and Carl." They'd teamed up with Daniel, and were circling him as they danced, getting closer and closer.

"If they get any closer, they'll need condoms," I muttered.

"Well, don't just stand there. Show them who's boss."

Just then the music changed, and Joe Jonas' voice filled the air, singing Cake By The Ocean.

That was all the push I needed.

I put down my glass, ran a quick hand over my hair, and smoothed down my shirt.

"Wait a sec!" Caroline grabbed hold of my neckline and tugged it lower, revealing more of my chest. Her eyes sparkled. "*Now* you're ready. Go get your man."

I kissed her cheek and picked my way slowly through the crowds to where Daniel was dancing between Max and Carl. I came to a stop in front of them, my heart pounding.

"I think this is my dance, don't you?"

Chapter 11

Daniel grinned. "I was wondering when you'd get over here. I was about to come and get you."

I gave Max a sweet smile as I eased myself between him and Daniel. "Thanks for keeping my place for me." I couldn't miss Daniel's loud chuckle.

Max blinked. "Oh… right." Then I gave Daniel my full attention, mirroring his movements until we were moving in harmony, edging closer to each other.

"And *there* you are," Daniel said with a smile that lit up his eyes.

"I've been here all night," I said with a shrug.

He leaned in close, and I breathed in his familiar scent. "No. That was some other Lee who was here to dance." He stroked my neck, and it sent shivers through me. "*This* is the Lee *I've* been waiting for."

I looped my arms around his neck, bringing our bodies into contact. I could feel the body heat radiating from him. He brought his hands to my waist, holding me close, moulding me to him, the pair of us moving as one, sinuous and sensual.

"You feel amazing," he murmured into my ear, before nuzzling my neck.

What I felt was *heat*, barrelling through me, electrifying my senses. And I knew exactly what I wanted in that moment.

"Kiss me?"

Daniel didn't hesitate. He claimed my mouth in a kiss that made me go weak at the knees. I curved my hands around the back of his head, wanting more, wanting him deeper, pulling him closer still. He slid his hands lower, until he was cupping my arse, holding me tight against him, so tight that I could feel the hardness he couldn't hide.

And then we were rocking together, a slow, sensual motion that left me in no doubt as to what he *wanted* to be doing right then. And didn't *that* thought send shivers trickling through me? I made an effort to breathe evenly, trying *not* to think about Daniel rocking against me, both of us horizontal, the feel of skin against skin. And still we kissed, our lips locked together just like our bodies.

It was the hottest fucking dance of my life, and I didn't want it to end.

The fire alarm splitting the air soon put paid to that.

The music stopped, and a voice came over the PA system. "Can we ask you to make your way out of the building, please? Just a precaution."

I gaped at Daniel. "You have *got* to be kidding me!" Someone somewhere was having a laugh at my expense.

My money was on God.

We filed out of the bar, along with the rest of the crowd, spilling out onto the street. Caroline and Troy came over to us.

"At least the sprinklers didn't go off," Caroline offered. She bit her lip. "Mind you, from where I was standing, it looked like you two needed a bucket of cold water throwing over you."

I gave her a hard stare.

The air had a chill to it, and Daniel handed me my jacket. "Well, the way I see it," he said, "we have three options. We either hang around here and wait for the fire brigade to arrive and check the place over, we go on to someplace else, or we call it a night."

"Except it's now officially morning," Troy added.

"I think the third option is out," I said. "Unless you really want to hang around Paddington Station for another five or so hours." I wasn't in the mood to find somewhere else—the fire alarm had killed that.

"I've got an idea," Caroline said suddenly. "Why don't you two come back to our place? You can grab some sleep there for a few hours. It beats trying to get comfortable on those seats at the station."

"Where do you live?" The idea of *not* sleeping at the station definitely appealed to me.

"We've got a flat about ten minutes' walk from here."

I opened my eyes wide. "You have a flat… in central London? What did you do, win the Lottery?" I chuckled.

Troy cleared his throat. "It's not a big flat. Caroline finds it easier to have a place in London during the week, for when she's working."

Daniel leaned in and said quietly, "She's a Human Rights lawyer."

Caroline merely smiled.

Okay, *now* I was embarrassed. It must have shown because Caroline kissed my cheek. "It's okay, sweetheart. I don't go telling everyone what I do when I meet them for the first time. And I was serious, by the way. You're both welcome to sleep on our sofa bed." She glanced at Troy. "I don't know about you, but I don't want to go anywhere else. I think I've had enough fun for one night."

Daniel looked at me. "Well?"

I rolled my eyes. "A sofa bed, or one of those hard-as-fuck metal seats at Paddington. Gee, let me think."

He laughed. "I think that's a 'Yes, we'd love to accept your kind offer, Caroline.'"

She beamed. "Great. Then let's get out of here."

I followed them through the crowd of

people who stood around talking, Daniel at my side. I was more than ready for a sleep if I was honest. It was only after we'd been walking for five minutes that Caroline's offer fully sank in.

A sofa bed. As in, *one* sofa bed.

Oh.

#LoveWins
love is love

Troy had been telling the truth—it *was* a small flat—but it had everything necessary to make it comfortable and functional. There was one bedroom, and a living room-cum-kitchen. The sofa bed was a double, thank goodness, and as Troy unfolded it and Caroline brought in pillows and sheets, I stared at it, trying to ignore my quickening heart.

It's just for a few hours.

We'll be asleep.

My intention was to be asleep the moment my head hit the pillow.

"Okay, the bathroom is through there," Caroline said, pointing to a door. "If you want anything to eat or drink, help yourselves." She smiled at us. "We won't be getting up before ten, so sleep in if you want. You don't have to catch the *first* train, right? Have a lie-in." And with that, she said goodnight and went into the bedroom, closing the door behind her.

She didn't say 'Have a lie-in *together'* but she might as well have done, because that was what my brain heard. And now it was just me, Daniel—and a sofa bed.

Daniel yawned. "I'm knackered." He gave me a grin. "Must have been all that dancing." He toed off his Skechers, removed his top in one agile move, dropped it over the back of the sofa, and proceeded to unbutton his jeans.

Oh God, I hope he's wearing something under there.

I turned my back to him and got undressed quickly, leaving my clothes in a neat pile on the coffee table. *This is ridiculous.* Less than an hour ago, our dancing had resembled nothing more than having sex upright, and now that we were about to share the same bed, I'd turned into my gran, who used to cover her eyes when there was any nudity on TV, saying things like, "Oh, my conscience,' 'Oh my,' and 'Don't look!'

Except part of me *wanted* to look. I *wanted* to see what Daniel looked like when he was naked. I'd already seen his chest—that just left the rest of him.

(And by 'rest of him,' yes, I mean the interesting bits…)

From behind me came the unmistakable rustle of cotton sheets. "I'm in bed. You can turn around now."

Damn him. I could hear the amusement in his voice.

I'd removed everything except my briefs. I hurriedly turned around, pulled back the sheet, and climbed beneath it. I forced a yawn. "I'm knackered too."

"I'll turn out the light, shall I?"

I didn't have to see his face to know he was smiling.

Fuck. "I'll do it," I said as I sprang out of the bed and sprinted over to the light switch. Then I was back under the sheet, my heartbeat racing.

"Lee?" Daniel whispered.

"Yeah?"

"I had a great time tonight."

The tension in my belly eased, and I relaxed. "So did I."

"Pity about the fire alarm. Just when things were getting… interesting."

Interesting? That had to be a euphemism for *hot as fuck.*

I waited to hear what else he had to say. Then I realized his breathing had changed, becoming more regular.

He fell asleep. How could he, when I'm lying here, waiting for him…?

What the hell was I waiting *for*?

With a sigh, I rolled onto my side, facing away from him.

Go to sleep, Lee.

#lovewins

love is love

June 17, 2018

I had no idea of the time when I awoke. From outside came the persistent drone of traffic, but inside the flat was quiet. Then I realized something was different. A warm body curled up against my back. A warm arm draped across my waist. Breath stirred my hair.

Damn, he feels good.

I lay there, not daring to move because I wanted to enjoy this. It had been a while since I'd shared a bed overnight with someone, and to be honest, it wasn't as if Cheryl and I had had many opportunities to do this. In fact, I think we only managed it a handful of times in the year we were together. She lived with her parents, and she hadn't been keen on staying the night.

Come to think of it, I hadn't been all that keen either. I mean, *think* about it. Would *you* want to bring a girlfriend home for the night, if you had four housemates? If we could all hear Justin having a wank in his room, then any… nocturnal activities would have required a gag to keep the noise down.

(Hey. *Hey*. Don't get side-tracked by the

gag remark. I'm not into that, okay? Anyway, back to my morning…)

"Morning." Daniel still sounded half asleep.

I turned my head to look at him, unwilling to change position. "Morning," I murmured. "You really crashed. One second you were awake…"

He gave an adorable little chuckle. "Sorry. Hope you didn't have anything planned."

I might not have done, but from the way my morning boner was trying to free itself from my briefs, it *definitely* had an idea.

When the thought occurred to me, I shivered. *I couldn't.*

My dick twitched.

But his hand is right there...

My dick twitched.

He can always say no, right?

My dick was inches from his fingers.

I kept my gaze focused on his face as I took hold of his hand and guided it to my erect cock. Daniel caught his breath. "Are you sure about this?"

I nodded, unable to get a word out. I shivered as he gave it a gentle stroke.

"So hard," he murmured, still keeping up that gentle stroking.

I groaned. "Daniel, for God's sake…" Then it was my turn to catch my breath as he reached into my briefs and curled his fingers around my shaft. I shuddered out a sigh. "Yes."

He slid his hand up and down my dick, slow as you please, until I was squirming. “Wait!” Daniel removed his hand instantly, and I reached under the sheets, grabbed my briefs and pulled them off as fast as I could, throwing them to the floor. Then I lay on my back, my erection tenting the sheet. “Now, where were we?”

Daniel chuckled. He rolled onto his side, propping himself up on one elbow, and once again he wrapped his hand around my cock. “I believe we were *here*.”

I shivered as he worked my shaft, unable to keep my hips still. He gazed at me like he’d never seen me before, his eyes wide. The firm hold he had on my dick was exquisite. But I couldn’t just lie there while he did his slow back-and-forth job on my cock. I reached up and stroked his chest, loving the shivers that rippled through him when I thumbed over his nipples, flicking the little bars through them.

He likes it.

Well, I could certainly work with that.

I played with his nipples, flicking them, tweaking them, and Daniel stifled a moan. Then I realized something warm and solid was tapping against my hip. His gaze met mine, but he said nothing, his lips parted as he pulled back on my foreskin, only to cover it again, the head of my dick playing peekaboo.

He’s not going to ask me, is he?

Go on. Make him feel good too.

I took a deep breath. "Daniel? Your dick is trying to escape your boxers. Take them off."

He stilled his hand. "Are you—"

"And don't ask me again if I'm sure, because if I wasn't, I wouldn't ask in the first place. Now take them off."

He let go of my cock, then reached under the sheets, wriggling for a second before slinging his boxers through the air to join mine. He lay back on his side, and I slowly slid my hand beneath soft cotton, my fingers encountering smooth, warm flesh.

For the first time in my life, I touched another guy's dick.

Daniel's long, drawn out sigh of pleasure was music to my ears.

"How do I … I mean, how do you like it?"

He smiled. "Pretend it's yours, and have at it." He pushed down the sheet, and I finally got to see his cock in all its morning glory. Okay, I've seen dicks before, but that was nothing compared to the sight of Daniel's, up close and personal. It was longer than mine, slim, with a nicely tapered head. And it was already leaking pre-come.

Come to think of it, so was mine.

"Lee?" There was a plaintive edge to Daniel's voice.

I rolled onto my side, and we negotiated the crossing of our arms as we tugged on each other's shafts, the pair of us achieving a kind of synchronisation as we moved our hands.

"Like that?"

Daniel nodded, his lips parted. "Oh, yeah. Just like that."

I couldn't resist the lure of those soft lips a moment longer. I leaned in, so did he, and our mouths met in a gentle kiss. Shivers ran through me as he kissed my neck, and my hand movements became jerkier. I tried to focus on pleasuring him as much as he was pleasuring me, but his mouth on my neck was a definite distraction. I rocked my hips, pushing my dick through his fingers, and he matched my movements, smearing the clear fluid down the shaft. Now we were making *sounds*, slick sounds, and part of me wondered if it that was what I'd hear when my cock was sliding into his hole…

Oh God. Just the thought was enough to bring me closer to the edge. *Can't think about that. Can't think about that.*

"Close," I warned him, my hips rocking faster, losing their rhythm as I neared orgasm. He nodded, his body's movement matching mine.

I wanted it to last. I wanted more. I wanted us to come together.

My dick apparently thought this was a race and crossed the finish line first. I pulsed spunk over his fingers, shuddering with each drop, and he groaned. It wasn't long before warmth covered my hand, and Daniel closed his eyes, his body jolting.

Watching Daniel come was… wonderful. *I did that.* And it brought a whole new dimension to wanking. *What do you know? Two hands are better than one.*

I lay there, getting my breath back, still holding onto his softening dick, his fingers still curled around mine.

Daniel met my gaze. "No regrets?"

"Only that it was over way too soon."

He laughed quietly. "I think we'd better clean up before they come in here." He glanced at the clock on the wall. "Wow. It's already nine o'clock."

"Seriously?" I must have slept really well.

"Lee…" Daniel's lips twitched. "You need to let go of my dick."

"I'll let go of yours when you let go of mine."

That got another laugh. Daniel let go with obvious reluctance and got out of bed to trot into the kitchen part, giving me my first glimpse of his arse.

Yup. Much better without the jeans. I liked the slight juggle as he walked. Then I wondered what on earth he was doing.

I soon found out when he returned carrying several sheets of kitchen roll.

"I was about to use my shirt to clean up with, until I realized I had to go home in it."

I snickered. "Yeah, that might get you a few

looks on the train." He handed me a couple of sheets, and I wiped up as best I could. I'd do a better job in the bathroom.

Daniel sat on the bed, watching me. "You have a nice body."

I smiled. "Thank you, but have you looked in a mirror lately?"

He huffed, as if to say *I have no idea what you're talking about.*

I like a modest man. I know these days you have to blow your own trumpet, but that's not me, and I can't stand people who brag. Daniel could've said, *Yeah, I know, I'm gorgeous*, but he didn't.

Like I said, modest.

He glanced toward Caroline and Troy's bedroom door. "Have we got time for a cuddle before they get up?" He gave me a shy look. "I can't just get dressed after that. I want to hold you. Is that okay?"

Naked cuddles… Another first, and one I wanted to experience. With him.

I nodded. He got back into bed, and I lay beside him, his body warm and firm against mine. Daniel put his arms around me, and we snuggled up. He smelled good, a mixture of his scent and spunk.

Oh, I could really *get to like this.* The weird part? I wasn't stressed about being naked with him. I guess once you've jerked someone off, that's not such an issue. I could forget about the fact that *I was lying naked in bed with a guy.*

Yeah, I might not have seen this coming—the whole being with a guy part—but now I was there, I liked it more and more. Not that I was going to think *beyond* that point, you understand.

One step at a time, right?

"This is nice," I murmured.

(God, I hate being so… *British* sometimes. I mean, *nice*? Couldn't I have used some other word? One that managed to more adequately convey how fucking *amazing* the experience had been?)

Daniel, apparently, had a better post-orgasmic grasp of vocabulary. He stroked my hair softly. "You look gorgeous when you come, you know. It's like you really let go, and I can see on your face how good it feels. I'm glad about that." He kissed my hair, and the sweet, intimate gesture sent a flood of warmth through me. Then he tilted my chin higher and kissed me, a chaste, gentle kiss that was absolutely perfect for the moment.

He cupped my cheek. "What are you doing for the rest of today? You don't have to go home right away, do you? Because I thought once we leave here, we might find a nice place, somewhere outdoors for lunch."

Lunch…

Oh fuck.

Chapter 12

I gazed up at the train information board. "At least it's on time." Even if it *was* the slow train. Unfortunately, Daniel wouldn't be on it with me: there was no stop at Newbury.

"Will you have enough time to get ready, then get back here to catch the train to your parents' place?"

"I think I might be a little late." In which case, they would have to lump it. I couldn't believe lunch had completely slipped my mind. But then again, my mind *had* been rather occupied, right?

Then I realized I'd be even later, because I'd said I was bringing wine. That meant a flying visit to the off-licence near the station.

The voice over the PA system announced the imminent arrival of my train, and Daniel sighed. "Will you call me tonight?"

I smiled. "Why—are you going to expire if I don't?"

Daniel's eyes twinkled. "I may not last the night."

"In which case, I'd better call you." I wanted him to kiss me, but something stopped me from asking. I wasn't sure what. If he'd been a girl, I wouldn't have hesitated, but then again, kissing a girl wouldn't provoke some nearby homophobe into giving me an arse-kicking. These days, you never know what's going on in some people's minds. *Some brave new world this is*.

Fortunately, Daniel was far braver than I was. He cupped my cheek and moved in for a gentle chaste kiss. "Thank you again for a wonderful evening. I'd like to say we could meet up during the week, but it's not going to be possible. I'll have rehearsals every night."

I widened my eyes. "That's a lot of rehearsals for just two numbers."

Daniel laughed. "We may only have two numbers on the stage, but we have ten to twelve songs planned for the route. That's one routine per song, and each one will get repeated three or four times during the day."

I hadn't realised how much work went into it. "Wow. You are going to be exhausted by the end of the day."

"And yet, I will be in Soho that night, surrounded by so many people from the LGBTQ community that you won't be able to slip a cigarette paper between us all. And Old Compton Street will look like a bomb's hit it when the day is over." He glanced at the board. "You need to go, or you're going to miss your train."

"Not until I have a final kiss." I guess his

bravery was rubbing off on me.

Daniel laughed softly and kissed me again, only this time, his lips lingered. “I can’t wait to hear your voice tonight,” he whispered before pulling back. “Have fun with your parents.”

I squinted at him. “That was a joke, right?” And with that, I made a dash for my train, not looking back. Once I was in the coach and in my seat, I took a moment to breathe. Saturday had turned out to be a pretty momentous day. I’d gone from ‘I’m straight,’ to ‘I’m not gay’ to ‘I’m bi’. I’d slept with a guy. Okay, so most of it had been *just* sleeping, but still… And that hand job this morning… Wow.

In the space of a week, my whole worldview had changed. What shocked me was how little it had taken for me to accept this shift in myself. Maybe part of the reason for that was the fact that those thoughts and feelings had always been there—I’d just had them on mute. Or maybe I’d ignored them. All I knew was, I was nervous, I was still excited, and I didn’t have a clue which way was up anymore.

#lovewins

love is love

“Sorry I’m late,” I said as Mum let me into the house. “My night ended a little unexpectedly, and I had to stay over at a friend’s house. It’s been a bit of a dash to get here.”

Mum chuckled. “Well, at least you’re here now.” Her eyes sparkled when I handed her the bag containing two bottles of wine. “Oh, we’ll never be able to drink all this.”

“Then put one aside for you,” I suggested. “You can have a glass when Dad’s on his beer.”

She smiled. “That’s a lovely idea.” She went back into the kitchen. From the living room I caught the tail end of a conversation about football between my dad and my brother-in-law, Ben. *Situation normal, then.* I avoided such conversations. I had no interest in football whatsoever, much to the disappointment of my dad. Now, put some *swimming* on the TV, and you had my complete interest. I would be glued to the screen, watching those lithe bodies propel themselves through the water.

(Okay, I know what you’re thinking. ‘And you really thought you were straight?’ Like I said, everything was on mute, and Daniel had just turned the volume up.)

I went into the living room to greet them. Dad gave me a warm smile. “How’s work? You still having to deal with ignorant arseholes?”

“Ah, so you’ve met the people I work with then?”

Ben chuckled at that. My sister Rachel was sitting on the couch, and I was struck by the tiredness in her expression. I sat beside her.

"Are you okay?"

She smiled. "I'm fine. It's good to see you."

This is where I should say that me and my sister get along really well. I always feel guilty because we don't keep in touch. But she has her life and I have mine. We need to call each other more though.

Mum bustled into the room. "Lunch will be in about thirty minutes. Now that Lee is here," she added with a glance in my direction. "So, *now* do we get to hear this news?"

Ben walked over to the couch and sat on the other side of Rachel. He took her hand in his, and that was when I knew something big was coming.

Please don't say you're moving, please don't say you're moving, please don't say you're moving...

Rachel smiled at Mum and Dad. "You're going to be grandparents." She glanced at me. "Which means you're going to be an uncle."

Mum erupted into a happy cry and my dad beamed. I can't say I felt the same. I think it was the fatigue that clung to Rachel.

Something's wrong.

I tilted my head to one side. "Then why don't you look like you're blooming? You know, the way most pregnant women look?"

Ben regarded me with approval. "I always said you were smart."

Rachel tightened her grip on Ben's hand. "This is our fourth attempt. The previous three ended in miscarriages."

Mum's face fell. "Why didn't you tell us?"

"Because you'd only have worried. Wouldn't you?"

Mum said nothing. Rachel had nailed it.

"But I had my twelve weeks scan a few days ago," she continued. "This is the farthest we've ever got, so fingers crossed…"

"Are you going to have to be careful?" I asked. She nodded. "But… it's not *dangerous* for you to continue, is it?"

Ben answered for her. "No, it's just that Rachel had a bit of difficulty making it… stick, so to speak. Hopefully, we're past that now."

I was happy for them. It was obviously something they really wanted. I'd never really thought about having children, but the idea of being an uncle appealed to me.

Yeah. You get to hand the kids back at the end of the day.

#loveWins
love is love

Dad poured a generous helping of gravy over his roast chicken and mashed potatoes, until his peas and carrots were swimming in it. “Now that’s *proper* gravy, like my mum used to make. You know, when you make it in the roasting tin with all the meat juices. None of this gravy granules nonsense *here*.”

It wasn’t as if that was the first time he’d said it. What made it interesting however, was the flush on my mum’s cheeks. Then I forgot all about gravy when Mum opened her mouth.

“So, Lee… are you seeing anyone?”

I’ll be honest, I didn’t know how to answer. I mean, I wasn’t ready to tell them about Daniel. “No,” I said at last, hoping that would bring an end to it.

My dad thankfully took the hint. “You won’t be able to move soon in London for rainbows everywhere.”

I blinked at the random turn of the conversation. “Excuse me?”

“That Pride thing. It’s this month, isn’t it?”

“It’s already started,” Ben volunteered. “It kicked off on the seventh, but the parade isn’t until the seventh of July.”

I’m not sure why Ben knowing that should be a surprise, but it was.

“Why do they need a Pride parade anyway?” my dad groused. “It’s just an excuse to prance around in the street, waving rainbow flags and carrying banners."

Ben said nothing. I wasn't going to let it go, however. "It's once a year, Dad. And *you* don't go anywhere near it, so it's no skin off your nose."

"But why isn't there a straight Pride?" Dad demanded.

Ben cleared his throat, his face tight. "Pride in what? Being straight? I'll tell you what. When straight people can get fired for being straight… when they can't give blood because they're straight… When they can't adopt because they're straight… Then yeah, *then* they can march."

I think I did well not to fall through the floor at that. Judging by my dad's expression, he was feeling the same way. No one spoke for the remainder of lunch.

Ben had gone right up in my estimation.

Rachel and I helped Mum clear the table, while Dad and Ben retreated into the living room to talk football, the previous conversation apparently forgotten.

But *I* hadn't forgotten it. I was seeing Ben in a whole new light.

I went into the kitchen to make the coffee, while Rachel loaded the dishwasher. The jar of instant coffee was almost empty, but I knew there'd be a new one in the cabinet. The surprise was the jar of gravy granules hiding at the back. I removed it and turned to face my mum with an expression of mock horror.

Mum paled. "Put that back where you found it. And you haven't seen it, okay?"

I brought my hand to my chest and gave a dramatic gasp. "He doesn't know, does he?"

She glared at me. "Of course he doesn't, but what he doesn't know won't hurt him."

I frowned. "Why the subterfuge?"

Mum pointed to the hob. "Remember when we changed the kitchen five years ago? Your dad wanted to swap the gas hob for an induction one."

I didn't get it. "And?"

She sighed. "With an induction hob, all the saucepans have to be magnetic, but there's no such thing as a magnetic roasting tin. And seeing as you make proper gravy by putting the roasting tin over heat while you add the flour and whatever, I couldn't do that anymore. So I've been using gravy granules ever since."

I grinned. "You rebel."

She laughed, then after giving the door a furtive glance, she lowered her voice. "You know what the best bit is? He tells me my gravy is just like his mother used to make."

Yeah, we both got a laugh out of that.

When the coffee was made, Mum took some in to Dad and Ben. Rachel gestured to me. "Come into the garden. Mum's been working there, and it looks really nice."

I followed her, the suspicion dawning that we really weren't going to look at mum's horticulture. I mean, seriously? Sure enough, once we were outside and as far away from the house as it was possible to get, Rachel stopped and turned to me.

"Okay, confession time."

I blinked. "Who's doing the confessing?"

"You are. When Mum asked if you are seeing anyone, you hesitated. That got me thinking. Because that could mean a couple of things. Yes, you *were* seeing someone, but you broke up. Yes, you *are* seeing someone, but it's not serious enough to share. Or yes, you *are* seeing someone, it's serious, but you don't want them to know for some reason."

Yeah, I could never hide anything from Rachel, even when we were kids. But I have to admit, as big sisters went, she was pretty cool—apart from the whole duck waddling remark.

I sighed. "If I tell you, you can't tell them."

Rachel stilled. "Of course," she said, her eyes wide.

We sat on the bench at the bottom of the garden, and I filled her in, from meeting Daniel on the train, to our date the previous night. And no, I didn't tell *everything*.

There are some things you don't share, even with your sister.

Rachel bit her lip. "Damn him."

I did the blinking thing again. "Huh?"

Rachel glanced towards the house. "Ben

said ages ago the reason you and Cheryl broke up was she discovered you were gay."

I smirked. "Well, he was wrong. I'm bi."

"The thing is, he was dying to set you up on a date with his brother Gary—who *is* gay."

I grinned. "Is he cute?"

She laughed. "Tell me about Daniel."

I'm not sure that after a week, I knew all that much about him. I told her about the dancing, what he did for a living, but I also told her he was kind, funny, intelligent…

I didn't mention that he was sexy as hell. You know, the whole sister thing?

"Is it serious?"

I stared at her. "It's been a week." Well, a little more than a week.

Rachel stared at me. "What difference does that make? I knew Ben was the one for me the day I met him. It took him a little longer to come to the same realization, but that's men for you."

I considered my previous relationships, if you could call them that. Cheryl was the only one I put in that class. "I'm fairly casual when it comes to dating."

"And does Daniel feel casual?"

I wasn't sure I could answer that. "He feels… different."

"When are you seeing him again?"

"I don't know. He has rehearsals every night this week for Pride."

"Are you going to watch him in the parade?"

I'd never even thought about it. "I don't know."

Rachel frowned. "Why not?" Then she grinned. "Now that you're the B in LGBTQA."

Maybe Rachel had the answer to my question of a week ago. "What do the Q and A stand for?"

"Q is for questioning," Ben said as he approached us. He came to a stop at Rachel's side. "A is for asexual. There's also I for intersex, but there's a lot more in there. Genderqueer, polysexual, non-binary, trans…" He gazed at me with interest. "Why are you asking?"

Rachel said nothing, and I was grateful for that. But I trusted Ben, especially after his outburst at lunch, and after learning his brother was gay. "Because your brother-in-law has finally worked out he's bi."

Ben's eyes lit up, and Rachel hit him on the arm. "And before you get any ideas about giving him Gary's number, Lee is spoken for."

I was about to contradict her, but I stopped. I liked the idea of being spoken for by Daniel. "I had no idea Gary was gay," I said to Ben.

He shrugged. "It's not something I'd share here." He glanced toward the house. "I love them, but sometimes…"

Rachel got up off the bench and laid her

hand on his arm. "They're not homophobic."

"No, they're not," Ben agreed. "Just a little ignorant of some things. And some of their attitudes are out of date." He glanced at me. "So if you're spoken for, when are you bringing him to meet them?"

I laughed. "For God's sake, give me a break. It's been a week."

Ben's eyes sparkled. "In that case…" He pulled his phone from his pocket and scrolled through, before holding it up to show me a photo of Gary. "To remind you what he looks like. You only met him once at the wedding."

I peered closely. "Damn. He *is* cute." We all got a laugh out of that.

"Hey." Rachel's eyes widened. "If a gay uncle is a guncle, does that make you a buncle?" She grinned. "I think I just invented a new word."

"And you're going to forget it, starting right now," I told her firmly.

I was *not* going to be Buncle Lee.

We stayed out there until Mum appeared at the back door, wanting to know if we were all going to miss the apple pie she'd forgotten to tell us she'd made. We trooped back to the house, Rachel's hand in mine.

"I hope it works out for you," she said in a low voice before we stepped inside.

"Me too," I replied.

What surprised me was how badly I wanted

it to work out. The whole Daniel thing might have been early days, but I liked the direction it was taking. And after that morning, I was in no doubt where we were headed. That by now familiar shiver skittered down my spine.

I'd had a taste, and I wanted more.

Chapter 13

When I arrived home late Sunday afternoon, my housemates were sitting in the back garden, soaking up the sun. *Garden* is a bit of a grand term, to be honest. It's little more than a patch of grass, with a table and chairs, and a tiny patio area near the door, but it's better than nothing. The small table was covered with empty beer cans, and all four of them were dressed in shorts and T-shirts.

Niall waved as I stepped out into the sun. "Hey, how was Sunday lunch with the parents?"

"It was okay." I smirked as I surveyed the scene before me. "All you need out here now is a barbecue."

Justin's eyes lit up. "That's a great idea. We could do that."

Mick coughed. "I foresee a slight problem with that idea." He gestured to the garden. "No barbecue."

Justin shrugged. "Duh. Then we get one. Even if that means disposable barbecues from the local petrol station. I've used those before. You just light a match and chuck it in. And I'm not saying we do it *now*—we give it a couple of weeks.

That leaves us time to find barbecues and get all the supplies in. Oh, and invite people."

Moz grinned. "Beer. That's all we need. Lots of beer."

"Some food might be a good idea," Niall suggested. "You know, hot dogs, burgers, chicken drumsticks, salad?"

"You were doing okay until you said salad," Justin said with a shudder. He pulled his phone from his shorts pocket and peered at the screen. "How about the last Saturday in June? That gives us a couple of weeks."

Mick opened his mouth as if to speak but shut it again. Moz and Niall were both grinning. Justin peered at me. "Feel free to invite who you like, but let's not go over thirty guests, okay? We don't want the place getting too messy or the party getting too rowdy. We might have neighbours calling the landlord and we don't want that."

"If it gets too noisy, it won't be the landlord they'll be calling. It'll be the police," Mick said with a twinkle in his eye. He glanced at Justin. "I'd better be in charge of the music. We all know how loud you play *yours*." That raised a few chuckles, while Justin stared at us indignantly.

"We can all chip in for the food and the beer," Moz suggested. "That's fair, isn't it?" We all agreed it was.

Niall glanced at the enclosed space. "Thirty people out here? I'd say more like twenty, tops."

"And the guests can bring a bottle too, can't they?" Moz suggested.

It looked like we were having a barbecue.

Watching them neck their beers was making me thirsty, so I went back into the house to find something for myself. I grabbed a can from the fridge and opened it.

Mick stepped through the back door, closing it quietly behind him. "He had to pick *that* weekend, didn't he?"

"Why? Do you have plans?" Then it hit me. "Are you seeing Pete that weekend?"

Mick nodded. "He's coming to London for a week, and he's booked us into a hotel. He wants to go to Pride."

I could see a cheaper option. "He could stay here," I suggested. "As far as anyone knows, he's a friend who's going to sleep on your bedroom floor. You don't have to tell them who he is."

Mick bit back a smile. "I see a flaw to that plan too. For him to stay here, I'd have to tell him we'd be… abstaining for a week, and I can't see him being happy about that. Not when we only see each other every three months or so." His eyes sparkled. "We tend to spend a lot of our time together in bed."

"Why would you need to—Oh. Forget I asked."

Mick laughed. "Yup. Let's face it. If one of us *farts* around here, everyone else knows about it.

So having sex? Forget it."

"I know it's nobody's business but yours," I began slowly, "but… you've been together for three years. Would it be so bad if you told the guys about him?"

Mick regarded me frankly. "And are you going to tell them about Daniel?"

"It's not the same thing," I stressed. "We've been on three dates—well, one real date, because the others were in his flat—which is nothing compared to the three years you two have shared."

"I don't know if I'm ready," he said in a quiet voice. "Hanging around with him in London, watching the parade, that's one thing. Having him meet this lot…"

I did get it. "Forget I said anything. It's your life, after all."

Mick cocked his head to one side. "So do I get to hear how Saturday night went? And more importantly, where you spent it? Because *somebody* wasn't in his bed last night."

"I wasn't in Daniel's, if that's what you're thinking." The thought was right there in my head. *But soon…* Sunday morning had taught me one thing.

Like I said, I was ready for more.

Mick gave me a thoughtful glance. "How is it going, really?"

From outside came the sound of laughter. "If we stay in here talking, they're only going to get suspicious and come and find us. Come to my room after dinner this evening, and we'll have a chat."

"That sounds serious."

I gave a wry chuckle. "I suppose it *is* serious, when you discover you've been hiding from the truth for a while."

"What are you two doing in there?" Justin yelled. "We're dying of thirst out here."

I rolled my eyes. "That didn't take long." I opened the fridge and grabbed more cans. There'd be time enough later to talk to Mick.

What I was really looking forward to was the conversation with Daniel that night, when I was tucked up in my bed.

I wanted to hear his voice.

"So how did lunch go?" Daniel asked.

I stuffed my pillow under my head and got comfortable. "I'm going to be an uncle."

"Oh, that's great. Congratulations. I'm never going to have that. Only child here."

That was the first time it struck me how little Daniel had shared about his family. I talked to him for a while about Rachel and Ben, about Ben's brother, my parents, in the hope that it would stir him to tell me about his family.

Nothing.

Finally, I went with a direct approach. “What are your parents like?”

“Oh, you know. They’re parents.” Yet more silence.

“Daniel?”

His sigh filled my ears. “I’m not giving away a lot, am I? There’s a reason for that.”

My heart sank. “I think I can guess.” It wasn’t exactly a unique story, right?

“I haven’t seen my parents since the day I left home at the age of seventeen.”

It was my turn to lapse into stunned silence.

“The long and the short of it is, they didn’t want a gay son, and I didn’t want to be in a family where I wasn’t wanted. So I left. End of story. I went to this charity that provides help for LGBTQ youth in need. They found me a place to live, a foster family… Ella and Rick are my parents now, even though it’s been seven years or so since I moved out. We’re still in touch. They helped me find a job. They gave me support when I needed it. So we are *not* going to talk about my biological parents again, okay?”

In that moment I ached for him, for the pain I couldn’t miss in his voice. “Okay.” In an effort to change the subject I told him about Rachel’s new word for me.

Daniel burst out laughing. “I love that! From the sound of it, I think I’d like your sister and brother-in-law as well.” There was a pause. “I meant to ask you… Saturday night… you and Caroline… From where I was standing at the bar, it seemed like there was a lot of soul-searching going on at our table.”

I smiled to myself. “Let’s say it was a night of revelations.”

“You looked so serious.”

I had to tell him. He was a part of this too, probably the most important part. “I’d just worked out I’ve been deluding myself all these years.” I didn’t want to talk about that, not right then. “We’re going to be having a barbecue here in a couple of weeks’ time.”

Daniel sighed. “I can’t remember the last time I went to a barbecue. Then again, I usually eat too much, and I spend the next few weeks trying to work it all off, so maybe that’s no bad thing.”

I wanted to invite him, but that wasn’t wise, was it? Besides, I was still finding my feet in a whole new world. Introducing Daniel to my housemates and any subsequent revelations to them—felt like a step too far out of my comfort zone.

I yawned, and he chuckled. “I think it’s time you were asleep. We’ve both got work in the morning.”

“Can we talk again tomorrow night?” I

asked.

His voice was warm. “Of course we can. I’d really like that. It might be a little late though. Can I call you at bedtime again?”

My words echoed his. “I’d really like that.” Part of me liked the idea of Daniel’s voice being the last thing I heard before I fell asleep.

#lovewins

love is love

June 18, Monday night

As soon as I was between the sheets, Daniel buzzed me. “Your timing is great,” I told him. “I was falling asleep on the couch. I figured it was time to do it in a bed.”

“Yeah, I know that feeling.”

I could hear the fatigue in his voice. “How was rehearsal?”

“Exhausting. There’s one song in particular with a really physical routine. Mac—he’s our troupe leader—is talking about rehearsing all next weekend. We’re only a few weeks away from the parade.”

“Rachel asked if I was going to go and watch you.”

“I’d love it if you could.” The sincerity in his voice was unmistakable. “It’s a lot of fun.”

"Even for you? From where I'm standing, it's a lot of hard work."

"Yes, it is. But… we work together as a team. We're not professionals, any of us—well, apart from Mac. He did this for a living. We're just there to have a great time, celebrating how far we've come and the fact that we can have a parade in the first place."

I recalled watching him on the dance floor. "You look pretty professional to me. I love the way you move."

"You're quite the mover too. Especially that last dance."

My face and chest grew warm remembering the way he'd held me against him as we swayed together. "Damn that fire alarm."

Daniel chuckled. "There's only so far we could have taken it, without attracting undue attention."

"I didn't want it to end," I confessed.

"When you grabbed my hand yesterday morning…" Daniel spoke quietly. "It was like you'd read my mind. I was lying there, trying to summon up enough nerve to touch you."

"Why didn't you?"

"I couldn't. It had to come from you. You're in the driver's seat." He sighed. "I keep second-guessing myself with you."

"What do you mean?"

"Take Saturday night. I was deciding what

to wear, and that included underwear. I had to choose between boxers or a pair of lacy briefs. Now, I'd have been happy wearing lace, but then I got to thinking… Why am I choosing them? Was it in the hope of being able to *show* you how I looked in them at some point? Because sleeping on Caroline's sofa was *not* in my plans. That was spontaneous. My only goal that night was to take you dancing and have some fun."

"And wearing lacy underwear felt too much like you were expecting something to happen?" I surmised.

Daniel's sigh of relief was obvious. "Exactly."

"Okay… Next time? Wear the lace. I want to see it." My heartbeat sped up.

"Really?"

I took a deep breath. "Confession time. The first time you told me about wearing such things, I found it so hard to keep my mind on the conversation." As soon as I said it, I realised how apt the word had been. I recalled being *very* hard at the time. "I kept picturing… your dick, trapped behind a layer of lace."

"Oh God."

"And I don't mind being in the driver's seat. Because that implies I get to decide where we're going."

"Am I going to like the destination?"

"Judging by how that dance was

progressing, oh, I think so."

Daniel made a happy little nose. "I like this, by the way. Talking to you last thing at night."

It felt like a good habit to get into.

"Sleep well, Daniel."

"Sweet dreams, Lee."

#LoveWins
love is love

June 20, Wednesday night

"Have you ever been in love?" I kicked off the duvet—the night was too warm for that. A cool, soothing breeze wafted in from the open window. Daniel's call had come in a bit later than I'd expected, and it was midnight. I'd dozed on my bed, waiting for him.

Daniel was quiet for a moment. "Where did that come from?"

"Just something I was thinking about today." I recalled Rachel saying she'd known Ben was the man for her the day they met. I couldn't imagine feeling so certain about someone. And then there was Gran. She used to tell me she'd known she'd wanted to marry my grandad when they were both fifteen. She said she then spent the next ten years working on him until he came to the right decision.

Yeah, my gran was quite a character.

Had I been in love with Cheryl? I knew I'd cared for her. But when she started talking about weddings and kids… I couldn't have been in love with her, could I? If I had, I wouldn't have ended it.

"I don't think I've ever been in love," Daniel said at last. "I think I'd know. I'm not talking about the earthshattering kind of love or anything like that. I'm talking about something *quieter*. A sure and certain knowledge that fills you. The feeling in your bones that this is him."

I smiled. "You're a romantic soul, aren't you?" Not that I was complaining. I thought it was sweet.

"I'm not denying it. Maybe that's why I'm not into one-night stands. I know so many gay men who are, and if it works for them, then fine. But it's not for me. I want a *connection* with someone." He paused. "What about you? Has anyone ever stolen your heart?"

Okay, that gave me a twinge of regret.

"Lee?"

I sighed. "I'd come to the conclusion that I didn't have one. A heart, I mean. Certainly, there's been no one who I felt I couldn't live without. I've had one serious relationship that lasted a year, but looking back, I keep thinking…. *Was* it that serious, or was I going along with it all? I just know it wasn't what I wanted."

"And what *do* you want?"

And there it was, the question that had plagued my mind that day.

"I want to *feel* something," I said at last. "I *want* that fluttery feeling in my stomach when I know I'm going to see them. I *want* my pulse to race when they walk into a room. I *want* my heart to bang away when we kiss. I *want* my skin to tingle when we accidentally touch, like there's electricity running through me. I *want* to get all tongue-tied when they're around me, because there's so much that I want to tell them, and I can't get the words out fast enough."

Silence.

"Daniel?"

He gave a soft sigh. "I think you just gave a perfect description of falling in love, and that's what *I* want too. All of it."

A lightness stole over me. *He didn't laugh at me.* He hadn't trivialized my feelings and desires. Better yet, he *understood* me.

"You know what really impressed me about you?"

My first reaction was stunned surprise. I don't think I've ever impressed anyone. And I'm not saying that to get an 'aw, poor you.' I mean it. I'm not an impressive kind of guy. There's nothing special about me.

Except… Daniel thought I could be someone special. He said so.

"I have no idea," I said after a moment's pause.

"The way you've… accepted all this. Me asking you out. Us dating. Making out. All of it."

"Well, what else did you expect me to do?" I was genuinely puzzled by his statements.

"Yes but look at how you did it. You didn't come out with some angst-heavy explanations about how you couldn't date me because you're straight. You said yes. You didn't make a big deal about it. It's as if… you simply accepted that this too was a part of who you are."

It took a moment for me to realize he was right. The crux of this situation was not sexuality but *connection*. A connection I was aware of the day we met.

I wanted to talk more, but I knew I'd regret it in the morning. I don't function too well on less than seven hours' sleep, and it was already past midnight. Thankfully, Daniel yawned, and I knew he too was tired.

Okay, and talking about feelings? I find that… challenging.

"We can talk more tomorrow," he told me, and I gave an internal sigh of relief. "But keep Friday night free? I'm thinking a DVD marathon and takeaway."

That sounded perfect. "I'll pencil you into my busy social calendar," I joked. Warmth filled me, and it was nothing to do with the temperature outside.

"Sweet dreams, Lee."

"Same to you, Daniel."

#lovewins

love is love

June 21, Thursday night

"I thought we could meet at Paddington. That is, if you can make the 18.04."

I'd make it, even if I had to sweet-talk she with the face like a slapped arse to ensure I got out on time. "Am I going home first, or am I coming home with you?"

"Well, that would give us longer for our DVDs," Daniel suggested. "And if tomorrow is as hot as today, you can always have a shower. I do have running water, y'know."

"Ooh, all the mod cons," I teased. Okay, the thought of being in Daniel's bathroom, showering… You *know* what I was thinking, don't you?

It seemed Daniel knew that too. "By the way… bring a toothbrush."

I stilled. "Oh?"

"Well, after what you said last time, about wanting to be prepared if you stay over…. Change of clothes, toothbrush… I'll make up the spare bed and you can stay the night. Makes more sense than us cutting short our night so you can catch the last train home."

Yeah, it sounded totally plausible to me too. So why was my heart beating like a bass drum accompanying a military tattoo?

Because staying over implied one thing—the possibility of sex.

And let's face it. After that weekend, it was less of a possibility and more of a probability. I knew it was coming, and I also knew I wanted it.

Okay, confession time. I'm a meat-and-potatoes kinda guy when it comes to sex, okay? So what if I'm very fond of missionary? And so what if all the girls I've dated so far also happened to be fond of missionary?

(Now that I think about it… were they *that* fond of it? Or was that the reason I didn't get past date #2 in most cases? Because I wasn't Mr. Adventurous in bed? Shit.)

"You've gone quiet on me."

I had to say something, right? I mean, I had to let him know what was on my mind.

"Daniel… I… I have no experience of gay sex, okay?"

"I kind of got that."

"No, what I mean is…" This was no time to be prudish.

He cleared his throat. "Are you trying to tell me you've never done anal?"

Thank God, he got it. "Nope, never. Apparently, I've been dating the wrong kind of girl," I replied, dead-pan.

There was a moment of silence before he burst into laughter. "Oh my God, that's funny."

I saw the funny side too and laughed along with him.

"Lee, it's okay, really," Daniel said in a low voice. "I meant what I said. You're in the driver's seat. We won't do anything if you don't want to."

I swallowed. "And… what if I *do* want to?" I whispered.

I caught the hitch in his breathing. "Oh."

Yeah. *Oh* pretty much summed it up.

"Let's just take this a step at a time, okay?"

I could live with that. "Okay." But I knew it *wasn't* okay. There was something niggling away at me. It had been since the previous night. "Daniel… you said you thought I could be someone special."

"And the more I get to know you, the more I know that to be true."

Fuck. He can derail me in a heartbeat. "It's just that…" I swallowed hard and bared my soul. "I… I don't want to… disappoint you." *Please don't let me have to spell it out?*

He didn't speak for a moment, and that only got my heart beating faster. "You could never disappoint me, okay?" His voice softened. "I can't wait to see you tomorrow."

And after that declaration, neither could I. "Yeah, me too. Good night, Daniel."

"Good night, Lee." He paused. "See you in my dreams."

I couldn't resist. "What kind of dreams will those be?"

He chuckled. "X-rated ones, of course." And then he disconnected.

I put my phone on mute and placed it on the bedside table, then lay on my back, the breeze from the open window pleasant against my warm skin. My mind was suddenly way too alert to sleep, and I toyed with the idea of getting on my phone and doing some… research.

Then I dismissed it. I knew what went where, for God's sake. And if I didn't try to get some shuteye, I'd look frightful by the time we met at the station.

Let's be honest, Lee. You need your beauty sleep.

My last thought as I fell asleep was that Daniel didn't—he was already beautiful, inside *and* out.

Chapter 14

June 22, 2018

My day was going to hell, and it was all Daniel's fault.

How? He'd set my mind on its present course with his casually uttered 'Bring a toothbrush.' That meant I'd started thinking about sex. And I carried *on* thinking about sex for most of Friday, damn him.

It had started out harmlessly enough. I'd gone to work as usual, only I couldn't stop thinking about the coming evening. Actually, I'd spent most of the night thinking about it too. I kept looking at my bag under my desk, where I'd packed my toothbrush, a pair of briefs and a T-shirt. The buzz of excitement and anticipation I'd awoken with didn't leave me all morning.

Then my first break arrived, and my mind went into overdrive.

I watched a colleague eating a banana. (Okay, I know, how terribly clichéd, but seriously, *you* watch someone slowly eating a banana, and try not to think dirty thoughts.) Then someone else came back from Sainsbury's with an orange Calippo, one of those ice lollies in the cardboard tube that you push up and suck?

Yup. As phallic as it sounds.

I could have coped with that, but it got worse as the day wore on. At lunchtime I went to the canteen to grab a bite to eat, but one look at the saveloy sausages, long and sleek and thick, sent my mind off on one of its little journeys, and I got out of there. I hurried next door to the Sainsbury's Express to buy a sandwich. A much safer option. Only, what was the first thing I saw as I walked through the doors?

Produce.

And before you think I've really lost it this time, we're talking courgettes. Big, *fat* courgettes with rounded ends. Aubergines, sleek and purple, as thick as my forearm. Cucumbers, so *very* long and in differing girths, all wrapped in clear plastic.

Which reminded me. I needed condoms.

I did my shop, chose a chicken mayonnaise sandwich, and headed for the cash desk. As I passed the bakery section, I couldn't help spotting the glazed ring doughnuts.

Okay, you *know* where my mind went that time.

Two women were standing in front of the cream cakes, pointing at them.

"Which do you prefer?" asked one of them. "I like the cream filled doughnuts."

"Oh, me too. But I love the cream horns. There's something about sucking out the cream that's really satisfying."

Christ, I *really* didn't need to hear that right then.

I went back to the office and dumped my sandwich on my desk. As I lined up for the coffee machine, I noticed the guys in grey overalls, carrying lengths of plastic piping. They were working on the A/C. (No wonder it was so hot in there.) I wasn't paying them much attention, but I caught snatches of their conversation.

"It's no good. I can't get the pipe to go into the hole."

"Then make the hole bigger, for God's sake. Find a saw."

I might have winced at that one.

"Never mind a saw. Just grease up the end of the pipe before you try it slide it in."

"Did you measure it? Because on the last job, they gave us the wrong pipe size, and no way would it fit in that small hole."

It was official. Somewhere, God was laughing his arse off.

I think if I could have spent the rest of the day with my eyes locked on my monitor and my fingers in my ears, I would have. Unfortunately, I wouldn't have got a great deal of work done, and having You Know Who on my back was the last thing I wanted or needed at that point.

I was going to be on that bloody 18.04 if it killed me.

Miracle of miracles, the remainder of my workday passed without any further incidents, but the damage had been done. I was trying not to think about the box of condoms in my bag. I'd debated *not* buying them, because surely, turning up with supplies was presumptuous, but in the end I caved.

Why bother being coy? I *wanted* this, right?

Mick had been correct all those days ago. I wasn't going into this because my sex life was lacking—I'd enjoyed sex so far. I wasn't looking elsewhere because I was tired of women. Far from it.

I was going into this because a gay man had made a connection with me, and I wanted to see what that spark would develop into.

By the time I got near Paddington Station, I was buzzing again.

Daniel will be there.

I'm going home with him.

I'm staying the night.

I know he said he'd make up the spare bed, but that was just for show, I was certain of it. We both knew where we wanted the night to end, and it *wasn't* with me in his guest bedroom.

Then I caught sight of him on the concourse. He was wearing the same pastel pink jacket and washed out jeans he'd been wearing the day we met. Daniel was scanning the crowd, obviously looking for me.

I couldn't help it. I dodged behind fellow

commuters, keeping out of sight until I reached him. Then I crept up behind him and tapped him lightly on the shoulder.

"Looking for someone?"

He swivelled around, his hand to his chest. "You almost scared the life out of me."

"Does that mean I've missed out on the chance of doing mouth-to-mouth resuscitation? Damn." I grinned. "Hello there. I'd give you a hug but I'm revoltingly sticky. I've been working in an A/C-free environment all day, so I wouldn't get too close if I were you."

"I'll settle for a kiss." Daniel smiled. "If that's okay."

It was more than okay. I leaned in, and our mouths met in a tender kiss. When we parted, Daniel took a cautious sniff, and I chuckled. "I *really* wouldn't do that."

He laughed, then shifted closer to whisper in my ear. "And what if I *like* how you smell?" When I blinked, he laughed again. "I could prove to you just how much I like it, but I think if I let you… feel the evidence, we'd be arrested."

"You are evil," I whispered back. He glanced at the bag over my shoulder, and I patted it. "Toiletries. Change of clothes." There was no way I was going to mention the condoms.

"Then let's get home."

As we headed for our platform, I tried not to look at his arse in those tight jeans. Because now

I was seeing it as it had been Sunday morning, bare, firm, and round.

I was learning something new about myself every day. Who knew I was an arse man? But now I wanted to do more than look. I wanted to touch. Stroke. Bite.

Then I remembered that first memorable episode of Queer as Folk: Nathan face down, while Stuart licked a path down to his hole.

Oh God. I couldn't do *that*—could I?

I shoved that aside hurriedly. *Not here.* Why thoughts of rimming Daniel should feel worse in the middle of Paddington Station, I'm not quite sure, but they definitely did.

We walked briskly along the platform, heading for the first coach. As per usual, there weren't many occupants, and we found seats with a table. I dumped my bag on it and sat next to the window. Instead of taking the seat facing me, Daniel sat beside me, his bag on his knee.

I was suddenly nervous, and I had no idea why. Maybe it was because he was sitting so close to me, close enough that his scent stole into my nostrils.

"What *is* that cologne you're wearing?" It was mellow, sweet, and a little spicy too.

It was also doing things to my dick.

"I have a friend who makes different colognes using essential oils. I have a couple of them. This one adds a little pep to my step."

It was certainly adding pep to *something*. "What's in it? Because it smells really good."

"Black pepper, sandalwood, coriander…"

I blinked. "You're wearing a herb?"

"The essential oil comes from the seeds." He laughed. "I'm sorry, but I had visions of me with coriander leaves hanging from my ears and in my hair." He leaned in closer. "Here. Take a good sniff."

I breathed him in, and I may have let out a sigh.

"That good, huh?" Daniel glanced around, then brought his lips to my neck. "How does it make you feel?" Then he kissed me there, soft and slow.

It was on the tip of my tongue to say, 'Horny as fuck,' but I didn't dare. We were on a *train*, for God's sake. "I think it's adding pep to *my* step too." Then I caught my breath when Daniel slid a hand across, hidden by his bag, and gently squeezed my crotch.

Okay, that was probably the hottest thing that had ever happened to me.

I stared ahead, not wanting to draw attention to myself, but my heart was pounding. There was no one nearby to see what he was doing, but that didn't mean a guard wasn't about to come into the coach at *any second* to check our tickets, right?

"You… you shouldn't be doing that," I

whispered.

Daniel's lips tickled my ear. "Do you want me to stop? Because it feels like you really like it."

Okay, talk about a dilemma….

Then I breathed again as he straightened and withdrew his hand. "I'm sorry. You're right. That was inexcusable. I can't think what came over me."

"And *I'm* sorry if that came across as a complaint," I remarked, my heartbeat returning to normal. "That was a first."

"Nothing wrong with firsts," Daniel observed. "Especially if they take us out of our comfort zone." He relaxed against the back of his seat. "That's what the troupe was for me at the beginning. I'd never thought I'd be dancing in front of hundreds of people, while wearing so little, and making such provocative moves."

I chuckled. "Okay, now I *really* want to watch you at Pride."

"It's two weeks tomorrow." Daniel's eyes sparkled. "Please come."

As if I could refuse when he looked at me like that. "Okay. I'll come."

He beamed. "Fantastic."

We settled into a comfortable silence, while I willed my cock to subside, because no way was I going to get off that train with a hard-on. It was bad enough that Daniel knew I was hard—I didn't want anyone else knowing. But having him so close, looking sexy with his reapplied lip gloss, his scent lingering in my nostrils…

It was all too much, especially on top of the day I'd had.

On top… Yup, my mind went there too, and not for the first time. Yes, I'd fantasized about sliding my dick into Daniel's mouth. Yes, I'd even thought about driving it into his arse, my fingers gripping his hips as I did it. But as for the whole concept of *not* being on top….

Had I ever played with my hole? No.

Had I ever *considered* playing with my hole? No.

Was I considering it now? *Oh God...*

Daniel nudged me, and I jerked my head to look at him. He grinned. "Don't you want to get off?"

Now that's *a stupid question.* Then I glanced through the window behind him as the train slowed, revealing the signs for Newbury Station. "Oh. Yes." I grabbed my bag from the table and stumbled to my feet, swaying a little as I followed him to the door.

Once off the train, we walked quickly through the throng of commuters, all of us heading for the exit. Three minutes later we were at his front door, and my heartbeat had resumed its now familiar hammering. We climbed the stairs, and I tried valiantly not to look at that fine arse, but by then I was a lost cause.

Inside the flat, Daniel hung his jacket on a hanger by the front door, and I dropped my bag to the floor next to the guest bedroom.

"I'll open the windows." He left me standing there while he hurried into the living room.

When I caught a whiff of myself, I wrinkled my nose. A shower was definitely in order. "Can I use the bathroom?"

"Sure," he called out. "There's a fresh towel on the bed in the guest room."

That was all the impetus I needed.

I opened the door, barely registering the light room with its double bed and lilac duvet, and grabbed the towel. Then I hightailed it into the bathroom, locking the door behind me.

The shower was wonderful, with forceful jets that energized me and left my skin tingling. I think I might have made it into the Guinness Book of World Records too, judging by how fast I was in and out of there. Daniel's body wash was a mix of jasmine and coconut milk, and it left my skin feeling silky soft.

I wrapped the towel around my hips, picked up my clothes from the bathroom floor, and unlocked the door.

"Feeling better?" Daniel called out from the living room. "I was going to ask if you'd had any thoughts on what you'd like for dinner."

I dropped my clothes on the guest bed, then

went into the living room, still in my towel. Daniel was standing with his back to me, peering at a DVD. He was still in his shirt and jeans, but his feet were bare.

I *really* liked that.

"I've got the extended versions of Lord of The Rings."

"Mm-hm," I murmured, walking up to him.

He turned round and stilled. He swallowed. "Or… there's The Hobbit trilogy."

"Mm-hm." I was close enough now that I could smell his gorgeous cologne.

"Or there's—"

I stopped his words with a kiss, my fingers fumbling a little as I unbuttoned his white shirt.

Daniel broke the kiss, his eyes wide. "Okay, that works too," he gasped, before taking my mouth in exactly the kiss I'd been craving.

There was no stopping me now.

Chapter 15

"Bedroom," I murmured into his kiss. Daniel opened his mouth, and I knew what was about to come from those soft lips. I stopped his words with a finger. "And before you ask me if I'm sure I want this…" I grabbed his hand and dragged it to my crotch, where my dick was already tenting the towel. "Does *that* feel like I want this?"

His eyes widened. "Who am I to argue with that?"

I grinned. "Sensible boy." I kept hold of his hand and led him to the middle door in the hallway. As we crossed the threshold, I remembered my bag. "I've got condoms," I blurted out.

"So have I." Daniel's eyes sparkled. "Great minds, and all that." He pulled me into the room, but as soon as we were inside, I pushed him against the door, his head thudding against the wood as I took his mouth in a blistering kiss. Daniel's hands were all over me, on my head, in my hair, down my back. I couldn't get enough of his kisses. I finished unbuttoning his shirt, and he tugged it free of his jeans, squirmed out of it, and tossed it aside. Then it was back to kissing, a fusion of lips and tongues.

He broke off, panting a little, and looked me in the eye. "Taking a moment to breathe here. And just so I'm clear? Who's doing what?"

My heart hammered. "Can I fuck you?" A surge of nervousness almost undid me. *This is really happening.*

His face lit up. "Thought you'd never ask." Then I gasped as he whirled me around, until it was *my* back against the door. Daniel yanked away the towel, dropped to his knees, and grasped my already hard dick around its base. He gazed up at me, his eyes reflecting the sunlit room. "Gotta get you ready, right?"

And then I cried out as he took my cock into his mouth.

Yes, I'd had blowjobs, so no, this wasn't new… and yet it was. This was *Daniel* sucking me off, and this was even better than I'd dreamed it would be. The friction was delicious, and my cock disappearing between his lips was something I would never tire of seeing. I held onto his head and made several short thrusts, careful not to go too deep.

He pulled free, his lips slick with saliva, and gazed at me. "You can go deeper, okay? You're not going to hurt me."

That was all I needed to hear. I placed the head of my cock to his lips and pushed, groaning as he opened for me and took me deep. I shuddered as he licked up the underside of my shaft before renewing his vigorous sucking, holding my dick steady with one hand while he rubbed his crotch with the other.

"Take it out," I demanded.

Daniel popped the button on his jeans, and I caught a glimpse of lace. Then he pulled his cock free and worked the shaft while he went back to taking as much of my length as he could into his mouth.

I don't think I'd ever been so hard. And I'd never wanted to be anywhere as much as I wanted to be inside him in that moment.

"Stop," I told him, before hauling him to his feet and kissing him like my life depended on it. He held onto me and I stroked down his back, sliding into his jeans, where my hands were suddenly full of soft, firm flesh. I slid a single finger through his crack, and he shivered.

He wasn't the only one. This was so new, and I wasn't sure my heart could stand the excitement.

"Ready for me?" I said between kisses. I had no idea where this boldness came from, but I wasn't about to question it.

Daniel's low moan was answer enough.

I released him, and grasping his jeans by the waist, I tugged them down over his slim hips, being careful to leave his briefs in place. His cock lay against his belly, trapped there by the lace panel that covered half his shaft. I trailed a finger over the knot of nerves under the head, knowing how much I liked it when someone played with my dick. Daniel shivered, and I didn't want to wait any longer.

"Condoms?"

He pointed to the bedside table drawer. "In there. Lube too."

I had them in seconds, but in that time Daniel had rid himself of his jeans. He got onto the bed on all fours, presenting that gorgeous arse, white lace stretched over his cheeks.

Okay. I'd never really thought about guys wearing lingerie, but my dick reacted instantly to the sight of that lace. It spread out over his cheeks, ending in a deep lacy waistband.

"This is so pretty." I could look at that all day.

"You know I said I wear lace to make me feel sexy?" Daniel twisted to look at me. "This time I wore it for you."

I bent over and kissed his arse cheek that wasn't covered by lace. I loved the way it accentuated his curves. It didn't hide his crease, however, and I rubbed the edge of my hand through it, loving how he groaned.

"You want me in there?" I slid a finger, pressing it between his cheeks.

"Yes," Daniel said with a moan.

I took hold of the lacy edge of the briefs, and eased the delicate garment slowly downward, leaving it just below the curve of his arse. I paused, gazing at his hole, watching as the puckered skin tightened and relaxed in quick succession.

"Lee." My name came out as an earnest plea.

I wasn't about to make him wait.

I removed the condom from its wrapper, unrolled it down my shaft, and then reached for the lube.

"Give me some too." Daniel held out a hand, and I squeezed some onto his fingers. Watching him reach back to slide a couple of slick fingers into his hole took me to a whole new level of hotness, and I was mesmerized by the sight—until Daniel gave a loud cough. He contorted himself to look at me over his shoulder again, and he was grinning.

"Is that a hint?" I tapped my gloved dick against his hole, and he shuddered. "Is this what you want?"

"Put it in me," he gritted out, shifting back until his knees were on the edge of the mattress, his lower legs hanging out over it.

I stepped between his legs and slid the head of my cock though his glistening crack, not wishing to tease him but loving the sensation. Then I positioned it against his hole and gave a gentle push. I gasped as his hole opened up and sucked the head it.

"Oh, fuck, yes, like that." Daniel bowed his

head.

My breathing rapid, I withdrew and did it again, and fuck, the second and third time the head popped through was just as hot as the first. When I'd done it about six times, Daniel let out a low growl, a sound I hadn't thought he had in him.

"Will you quit teasing and just *fuck* me?"

Never let it be said I can't follow instructions.

I repeated the action, keeping my movement slow, my shaft going a little deeper each time. With each penetration, Daniel moaned a little louder, but kept still, leaving the depth up to me, until at last I was all the way inside him.

Fuck, it was tight.

It was *gloriously* tight.

It was heaven.

I slowly pulled out of him, only to slide back at an equally leisurely rate, taking my time, letting his body adjust. After a few minutes of this, I picked up a little speed, driving my dick a bit deeper, my hips rocking.

"Lee. I can't stay still."

"Then don't," I flung at him, grabbing his hips and holding on as I began to fuck him in earnest. Daniel started rocking back and forth, meeting my thrusts, and we soon got into a rhythm. I yanked him back onto my cock, spearing him with it, filling him to the hilt, and Daniel pushed back hard, impaling himself over and over again.

"Aw, fuck, yes." Daniel's breathless praise only spurred me on to fuck him harder, and our bodies met in a loud slap of flesh on flesh. My hips snapped forward as I drove into him again and again, my gaze locked on the sight of my dick burying itself in his hole. Sweat dripped from me onto his back, spattering in little starbursts of moisture.

When my body tingled and electricity zapped all the way through me, right into my balls, I wanted to weep with frustration. I'd known it wouldn't last long, of course. I was too close to have any outcome other than an early finish. "Sorry," I gasped out as I came. I covered his body with mine as I clung to him, my head on his shoulders, my arms around his waist while I filled the condom, my cock buried deep inside him. Daniel stilled beneath me, and I wondered if he was as disappointed as I was with the premature end.

Okay, so it wasn't over *that* fast, but still.... I'd wanted the experience to last.

Gingerly, I withdrew my half-hard dick, holding onto the condom which I removed carefully, tying it up and placing it on the floor beside the bed.

Daniel rolled onto his back, his fingers curled around his cock as he tugged at it, his hand a blur. His neck and chest glistened with sweat. Then he cried out as he shot his load, coating his chest and chin with it. I waited until he was done before lying on the bed beside him. His body trembled, and I stroked his damp chest. Both of us had worked up a sweat, which wasn't surprising given the temperature outside.

He cupped my head and pulled me down into a long, fervent kiss. I didn't give a fuck that our bodies were slick—I clung to him as we kissed, desperate to hold onto that connection.

When he released me, Daniel looked me in the eye. "You said sorry." I nodded. "But what on earth for?"

I gazed at him with wide eyes. "Because it didn't last. Because we only managed one position." *Because I'm no good at this*, I said silently.

Daniel blinked. "You're serious." And before I could utter another word, he flipped me onto my back, his weight on top of me. "Now listen to me. I don't care if it lasted five minutes or five hours—you felt amazing inside me." His lips twitched. "Personally, I'm glad it didn't last five hours, because I don't think I'd be able to walk for the next week if it did. And as for one position…" He gave me a quizzical look. "What were you expecting?"

"Well, I'm bloody sure there are more positions than just doggy style. I… I wanted to make it good for you." The words came out louder than I'd intended.

Daniel took my face in his hands. “Did you enjoy it?”

“Yes—what there was of it.”

He sighed. “Forget how long it lasted—how did it feel?”

My sigh echoed his. “Amazing. You were so tight… I could have done that all day.”

Daniel chuckled. “And when *I’ve* finished with you, cutie, you’ll be going half the night.” He kissed me. “You know what they say. Practice makes perfect.”

“I take it we’re going to be doing more practicing?” My heart felt lighter at that.

“If I had my way, we’d be practicing all the hours God sends. And as for making it good for me…” Daniel kissed me again, a slow, toe-curling kiss that sent waves of pleasure through me. I loved how it felt to have his weight on me, pinning me to the bed. Daniel broke the kiss and locked gazes with me. “I loved every second of it, and I can’t wait until we do it again.”

My stomach rumbled, and I groaned inwardly.

Daniel laughed and sat up beside me on the bed. “I think that’s our cue to eat. I was asking about that, if you recall, before you had your wicked way with me.”

“Do we have to go out?” It was way too hot to put on clothes.

Daniel smiled. “I think I’ve got enough in

the flat to feed us. How would you feel about a picnic dinner in bed?" He pointed to the TV sitting on top of the chest of drawers. "We can even have our DVD marathon while we eat."

I grinned. "Will we get commercial breaks?"

"There *are* no commercial breaks on—" Daniel's eyes gleamed. "Oh. I see. I think that can be arranged."

"There *is* one thing I'd like to ask before we eat."

"Ask away."

I gestured to my sticky body. "Would it be okay if I took another shower?"

"Of course. But only on one condition." When I gazed at him inquiringly, Daniel smiled. "The management reserves the right to be present while a guest showers. And this might include actually being *in* the shower at the same time as the guest. For health and safety reasons, of course," he added with a straight face.

"Oh, of course," I replied, equally seriously.

Daniel climbed off the bed and held out his hand to me. "Then let me escort you to the shower."

I smiled as he tugged on my arm, pulling me to my feet.

Another first.

Chapter 16

"I love these films," Daniel said as the credits rolled for *The Fellowship of the Ring*. "I've lost count of how many times I've watched them."

I couldn't resist. "So which one of them are you watching it for—Orlando Bloom or Viggo Mortensen?" I was relaxed, which was fairly amazing given the circumstances. We hadn't got dressed after the shower—and before you ask, all we did was wash each other. For a long time. Thoroughly.

Until the water ran cold.

Anyway, we were lounging on the bed naked, having watched the film in that state. I was never one of those people who enjoyed strutting around starkers, but I had to admit, it was kind of liberating. I'd thought I'd be forever looking at him, at his dick, but I wasn't. And as the film progressed, I grew more and more comfortable.

It was turning out to be a bumper night of firsts.

Daniel gave a mock gasp. "Are you implying I'm only watching these films to drool over hot guys?"

"Yes," I replied instantly. "So which one?"

My money was on Viggo. When Daniel's cheeks flushed, I was intrigued. "Come on, confess."

He stared at the duvet. "Elijah Wood."

I stifled a chuckle. "I see. Got a thing for hobbits, have we?"

Daniel jerked his head up and stared at me. "It's those eyes! And that hair. He is *seriously* cute. I'll take cuteness over rugged good looks any day." Daniel's eyes sparkled. "Which is why there's a cute man in my bed right now." He removed the plate that had contained pitta bread, hummus, raw vegetables, grapes, and sour cream dip onto the bedside table, and then gazed at me.

There was definite intent in those beautiful eyes.

"What are you up to?"

Daniel gave me an innocent glance that didn't fool me for an instant. "I'm just tidying up."

"Mm-hmm." I gestured to the TV. "Are we watching the next one, or what?" My heartbeat didn't think so. It picked up speed.

"Or what," Daniel said with a grin. "Commercial break time."

I had a feeling he knew exactly what he wanted to be doing during the break.

Okay, so I had ideas too. It was just a matter of who got to act on theirs first.

"Can I ask a personal question?"

I bit my lip. "Considering I was just inside you, I think you can ask whatever you want."

That's about as personal as it gets, right?

Daniel knelt on the bed in front of me. "Did any of your girlfriends ever play with your arse during sex?"

I blinked. "Wow. You really meant personal, didn't you?" Not that I minded. "And the answer is no."

"Have *you* ever played with it? With toys, or maybe just a finger?"

I went with honesty. "No." I paused. "But I've been thinking about it lately. Especially after—" *Nope. Nope. Nope.*

Daniel arched his eyebrows. "Secrets already?" He stroked my thigh.

Why did he have to go and touch me? There was something about the feel of his hands on me that scrambled my brain. I couldn't think straight.

(Yeah, I know. Not straight. I got the memo, thank you.)

"Tell me." It was a simple entreaty, and one I couldn't ignore.

I took a deep breath. "Remember I said I was doing some 'research'?" I air-quoted.

He nodded. "Queer as Folk." Then he stilled, and his eyes lit up. "You saw something that you wanted to try, didn't you?"

I caught my breath, unable to get a word out.

Daniel regarded me with obvious amusement. "Well, if you don't tell me, I can't bring your fantasy to life, now can I?"

Oh fuck.

I swallowed. "First episode. Nathan and Stuart. He… he was licking…"

Daniel's lips parted, and a soft sigh escaped. "Oh, I think we can do something like that." He shifted forward, placed his hands on my thighs, and gently pushed them apart.

"Daniel…" Fuck, my heart was pounding.

"Relax," he said in a soothing voice. "I just want to get as close to you as possible while I kiss you." Then he gently tugged on my hips until I was lying down, my legs spread wide, before lying between them. I welcomed his weight on me, his kiss, and I wrapped my arms around him, holding him against me.

Kissing Daniel was always a joy.

Kissing Daniel naked took that joy to a whole new level.

We moved with each other, the motion gentle and unhurried, and with each kiss I felt more connected to him than ever. I stroked the back of his head, his shoulders, his back, and then slid my hands lower, wanting to feel the swell of his arse. Daniel broke the kiss and shifted a little higher, and I squeezed his cheeks, pulling them apart, loving the soft groans that left him.

He shifted again, and our lips met in a lingering kiss before he laid a trail of kisses down my neck to my chest, pausing at my nipple. He raised his chin to look at me, then lowered his head and flicked my nipple with his tongue.

It was as if he'd flicked on a switch, and my body lit up.

I shuddered, both hands on his head as I held him there, wanting more of the exquisite sensation. I pointed to my other nipple. "This one is feeling a little neglected," I managed to get out.

Daniel chuckled against my chest, and it tickled. "Oh really? Well, we can't have that, can we?" He licked a path between them, and I groaned when his warm mouth enclosed it, sucking on it and flicking it. Then he was moving again, kissing a trail down my torso, pausing to dip his tongue into my navel, before reaching my cock.

I grasped it around its base and rubbed it slowly against his cheek and chin.

Daniel's eyes gleamed, and he kept his eyes locked on me as he ran his tongue along its length from root to head, then repeated the action in reverse until he reached my balls.

He paused, and I wanted to scream with frustration. He held out a hand. "Pass me a pillow?"

I grabbed one and gave it to him. Daniel stuffed it under my arse, lifting it slightly. Then he lay on the bed between my legs, his face inches from my crotch.

"Grab your legs and hold them against your chest."

I blinked. “We’re not all as lithe as you, Mr. *I Dance In A Gay Man’s Dance Troupe.*”

He laughed. “It’s easy. Just grab your knees and hold onto them.”

I snorted. “What is this, choreography, or a desire for me to become some sort of contortionist?” My money was on the latter. Then I forgot my witty comebacks when Daniel rubbed a finger over my hole. I shivered.

Daniel paused. “Good shiver or bad shiver?”

“It was a ‘do that again’ shiver, if you must know.”

So he did it again, and damn, I didn’t want him to stop. Then he moved in closer, until I could feel his warm breath on my hole.

I gave a shudder. “Please…”

Daniel gently spread my cheeks, and the feeling of warmth there intensified. His gaze met mine. “Just so you know? I don’t do this often.”

I swallowed. “Why not?” Was he about to tell me he wasn’t going to do it with me either? My pulse raced.

He hesitated, as if he was debating whether or not to share. Then he drew in a long breath. “Because for me, rimming is something I only do when there’s a profound connection between me and a lover.”

And before I could ask if *we* shared such a connection, Daniel licked a leisurely path over my hole.

If I'd thought my body lit up when he played with my nipples, it was now experiencing a power spike of epic proportions. I groaned out loud, and he did it again, only slower this time, pausing to press the tip of his tongue against my pucker. Then he licked again, from my hole to my taint and back again, taking his time.

"Oh fuck, Daniel."

"Is that Lee-speak for 'don't stop'?"

I let go of my legs, reached between my spread thighs and grabbed his head, keeping him there.

Daniel's only response was to lick again and again, and with each pass of his tongue, I thought my head would explode. He stroked my arse while he kissed and licked, and I suddenly knew what he meant.

This was intimacy.

"Please, don't stop." The words came out as a whisper.

Daniel gently pulled on my cheeks, stretching my hole wide, before pushing the tip of his tongue against it. He did it again. And again. And again, only this time the tip penetrated a little deeper, and I gave a low moan.

It seemed to be the signal Daniel was waiting for.

He pushed his face into my crack, his tongue in my arse, and ate it with abandon, his own noises speaking of the pleasure he got from it. I couldn't lie still a second longer. I grabbed my knees and tilted my arse higher. Then I settled into a rocking motion, crying out from the sensations as Daniel licked, flicked, sucked and penetrated, bringing fingers into play, alternating between finger and tongue, until my dick stood upright, solid and aching, and I knew I could come without a single touch to it.

Then Daniel knelt up. "Can't get my tongue in deep enough like that." His lips were slick with saliva. Before I could draw breath, he grabbed my arse, rolling it even higher up off the bed, then dove back in.

I was bent in half, almost performing a shoulder stand, my knees were at my ears, and Daniel was fucking me with his tongue. Every nerve ending down there was alive, sending shocks through me that tingled and jolted me. His fingers dug into my cheeks as he pulled them apart, stretching my hole even wider. The feel of his tongue in there was driving me to the edge, and I went with it, my body trembling, clutching my knees and shaking as Daniel picked up the pace.

"Gonna come," I warned him. There was no stopping *this* train.

Daniel let go of me, and I lowered my legs, wrapping my hand around my cock and holding it against my belly as I shot hard, my body shaken by the force of my orgasm. The top of my head came off when Daniel's mouth enclosed my dick, and waves of pleasure crashed over me as he cleaned up every last drop, then licked what was left from my chest and abs.

I pulled him down into a kiss, clinging to him as my body rode out the last mini shocks from my climax. I could taste my cum on his lips, his hands were gentle as he stroked my face and neck, and my head was still reeling. I couldn't speak. I wouldn't have known what to say if I could.

Mind officially blown.

Daniel rolled onto his side next to me, his gaze locked on my face. "So did reality live up to the fantasy?"

A number of replies flitted through my brain.

Do you have to ask?

Couldn't you tell?

But I ignored them all. This was no time for a light-hearted comment. I cupped his cheek and looked him in the eye. "You just shook my world."

I meant every word.

Daniel's breathing hitched. "Thank you."

I chuckled. "I think that should be my line."

He leaned in and kissed me. "You *are* going to sleep in here tonight, aren't you?"

My quick-fire brain kicked in, but I reined in my mouth before I could say 'Well, actually, I was going to sleep in the guest bedroom.'

"I can't think of anywhere else I'd rather

be," I replied. We might have shared a bed before, but I knew this night would be different.

I wanted to fall asleep in his arms.

Judging by the way his face lit up, Daniel felt the same. "Then how about a quick clean-up before bed?"

"No more Lord of the Rings?" I said with a teasing pout.

He laughed. "We can watch the next one tomorrow night—if you'll stay till then?"

"I'll stay," I assured him.

I couldn't think of anywhere I'd rather be.

Chapter 17

June 23, 2018

Waking up in Daniel's bed was light-years away from the previous weekend.

His arm was draped over my waist, just as it had been in Caroline's sofa bed. His breath stirred my hair. What made it different was the warm bare cock that pressed against my arse, and the feeling of happiness that filled me as I lay there.

He still feels good.

Soft lips nuzzled my neck, and I shivered. "Good morning."

"It is when I wake up with you." He snuggled closer, his cock like a brand, hot and hard. "It's still early."

I turned in his arms, and his lips met mine, our arms enfolding each other. Daniel hooked his leg over mine, pulling me in, and his dick dragged over my morning wood. He gave a sleepy smile. "And I thought *I* was hard first thing in the morning."

I chuckled. "Whatever shall we do about that?" When he didn't respond, I wasn't surprised. Daniel wasn't going to push me into anything. And so far, sex had been pretty one-sided, and that didn't strike me as fair. Equal opportunities, right?

Time for another first.

I rolled him gently onto his back, then glanced down to where his cock lifted the sheet. "I think I need to take care of this, don't you?"

Okay, *that* got him breathing faster.

"You don't have to," he said earnestly.

I cut off whatever else he was about to say with my finger to his lips. "And what if I want to?" Because deep down, I truly did. I wanted to know what he tasted like, how he'd feel in my mouth…

"We could help each other out," he suggested when I removed my finger.

I shook my head. This was *my* turn, and I wasn't sharing it with anyone. Besides, I suspected me blowing Daniel while he blew me would bring everything to a *very* swift conclusion.

He threw back the sheet, and his dick pointed toward the ceiling. I laughed. "*Someone* is eager."

"Can I touch you while you do it?"

As if I'd refuse him. "Of course you can." I knelt beside him, bent over his crotch, and took his cock in my hand. I wasn't going to ask for instructions—I knew what felt good for me, right?—but I did want him to enjoy it.

No teeth. No teeth. No teeth.

(Yeah, been there.)

Daniel took my hesitation for reluctance. "You don't have—" Then he groaned as I circled the head of his dick with my tongue. He laid his hand on my hip and stroked me there, and I lowered my head, taking as much of his shaft into my mouth as I could fit without choking. I slid my lips up to the tip, then took him deep again. His cock was so warm, his foreskin so silky. There was no taste to speak of and having my mouth full of him was a turn-on.

"Oh, God, that feels amazing."

I wasn't looking at Daniel's face—my attention was focused on the long, slim dick in my hand. I couldn't take it all, but I did my best, sliding my lips up and down his shaft, building a little speed. Now and again, I licked his cock from root to head, because that never ceased to feel damn good when *I* was on the receiving end. I pulled free of him and worked his slick length with my hand before resuming my erotic task.

When Daniel squeezed my arse cheek, I moaned around his cock. I bobbed my head up and down on his dick, loving how he made little movements with his hips, clearly trying to limit his thrusts. But he completely threw me when he rubbed a slick finger over my hole.

I'll be honest. That stellar rimjob the previous night had opened my eyes, and I knew if he asked to fuck me, I'd say yes, because I wanted to know how it felt. His tongue in my hole had been glorious—I couldn't imagine his cock feeling any less amazing.

My dick was hard as nails but I ignored it. This wasn't about me. It felt sloppier than any blowjob I'd received, but if the sounds that poured from Daniel's lips were anything to go by, he wasn't complaining. In fact, he dug his fingers into my arse cheek and his breathing sped up. I knew he was close, so I worked his shaft up and down with one hand, while I sucked hard on the head.

His cry of pleasure erupted about a second before he did, and his load spattered my lips and cheeks, narrowly missing my eyes. Daniel ignored my now sticky face, and pulled me in for a kiss, pushing his moans between my lips as he held onto me, his body wracked with tremors. In that moment, I felt like I could conquer the world.

Daniel gazed at me with wide eyes. "If that was your first time…"

I laughed, and that powerful feeling of invincibility flooded through me. "I think there's still room for improvement," I teased, bringing my fingers to my face. "For one thing, I seem to be wearing a lot of you. Maybe I should aim for more of you in my mouth next time."

I had never felt more alive, more vital than I did in that moment. And I knew it was because of Daniel. It wasn't just the sex, the rush of endorphins…

It was him.

#loveWins
love is love

When I caught sight of the sign through the window of the taxi, I gasped. "I know you said it was a surprise, but I never expected this."

Next to me, Daniel chuckled. "When I found out you were a fan, I knew we'd have to come here, especially as it's only five miles from me."

A mystery tour, he'd said that morning.

A secret, he'd said.

He hadn't even said our destination out loud when we got into the taxi outside his flat, but had handed the driver a piece of paper. I'd laughed at all the subterfuge.

And now I was standing in front of Highclere Castle, the sky a startling shade of blue above it, not a cloud to be seen. The castle was every bit as impressive as it was on the TV screen.

"Well?" Daniel demanded. "Good surprise?"

I laughed. "No—an excellent surprise." I gave him a huge smile. "Thank you." It was the perfect way to spend a beautiful summer's day, visiting one of the most iconic castles in the UK. Daniel had brought a picnic for our lunch, and told me we'd have it in the gardens. But the first thing I had to do was stand in that famous courtyard.

"I keep waiting for Carson and Mrs Hughes to come out," I murmured. "And for all those gorgeous cars to drive up, with Lord Grantham, Lady Grantham…"

Daniel laughed. "Do I have to explain that Downton Abbey is fictional?"

I gave him a hard stare. "Only if you want me to be really unhappy." Inside, I was buzzing. He'd chosen this destination for *me*. We'd discussed Downton Abbey a few times since we'd been dating. I was delighted to learn he was a fan too, especially because it made me feel less of a geek. My housemates were of the opinion that I was weird, because how many guys my age would confess to liking a historical drama?

"Can we go inside?"

Daniel chuckled. "Do you really think I'd bring you here if all you could see was the gardens? There's a tour. We get to see the main state rooms, some of the bedrooms and the cellars, and downstairs in the old staff quarters there's an Egyptian Exhibition."

I blinked. "Really?"

"The castle is owned by Lord and Lady Carnarvon now, but the 5th Earl discovered the tomb of Tutankhamun, with a bit of help from Howard Carter, of course."

I had to smile. Daniel was every bit as geeky as me.

The guided tour was fabulous. Standing in that main hall, looking up at the gallery, staring at the beautiful staircase and imagining Lady Mary sweeping down it on her wedding day…

I was in heaven.

"I'm just as bad as you," Daniel murmured as we followed our guide into the state room, where so many banquets had taken place. I could almost hear Maggie Smith, uttering one of her acerbic comments.

"What do you mean?"

He let out a wry chuckle. "I keep expecting to see Thomas, standing with his back to the wall, in his footman's livery."

"I know he was the bad guy, but I couldn't help feeling sorry for him." I'd been overjoyed when they'd announced there was to be a film version, due for release the following year. "Do you think they might possibly plan a happy ending for him in the film?"

Daniel huffed. "A happy ending? For a gay character in those times? I doubt it."

"I can dream," I said with a shrug. Then I gave our guide my full attention as she pointed out some of the portraits hanging on the walls.

By the time our tour had ended, I was more than ready for lunch.

Daniel chuckled. "Save some room. We have high tea still to come."

Okay, that was the icing on the cake,

literally. I was going to have high tea at Downton Abbey.

We wandered out into the gardens, and as soon as I saw the columns at the far end of the property, I pointed them out. "There. Let's eat there."

Daniel laughed. "Yes, Lady Edith."

"Oh, funny man."

We walked slowly across the grass, and when Daniel took my hand in his, I felt as light as air. I glanced down at our joined hands, and warmth filled me.

I'd never seen myself as romantic. I wasn't one to get emotional. But somehow Daniel had gotten under my skin. I recalled watching the DVD the previous evening. We'd sat on his bed, leaning against a mountain of pillows—and each other. I couldn't recall ever feeling so comfortable with someone, and I had to admit, I liked it.

We sat next to the temple, looking out over the grounds, the castle rising majestically at the centre of it all.

"This was a great idea. Have you been here before?"

Daniel shook his head. "I guess I was waiting until I could share the experience with someone. Looks like that someone was you."

I chuckled. "Do you always know exactly what to say?"

Daniel laughed. "What can I say? It's a

gift."

We ate our sandwiches in silence, while the sun shone and the birds sang. As picnic spots went, it was idyllic.

"You're sure I'm not taking up your Saturday?"

I laughed. "Oh yeah. You're keeping me from my laundry." I peered at him. "I thought you had rehearsals this weekend."

"Someone persuaded Mac we could get it all done in five hours on Sunday afternoon, so I got a day off."

"And you spent it with me. I'm touched."

Daniel chuckled. "You were certainly touched this morning. All over, as I recall. And I plan on doing the same thing tomorrow morning too."

I arched my eyebrows. "I take it I'm staying another night with you?"

"If you want to."

I shifted closer, until my thigh was snug against his. "Of course I want to." I looked him in the eye. "Do you think the tourists will be offended if they see us kissing?"

"Why don't we find out?"

My hand was on his neck as I closed the gap between us and kissed him on the mouth, slow and easy. I didn't bother keeping it chaste: despite my question, there was no one near enough to take offense. And sitting beside a mock ruined temple in the afternoon sun, kissing a gorgeous man, was my idea of a perfect Saturday.

What made it even better was the prospect of spending another night in Daniel's bed. Because I had a feeling not all of it would be spent sleeping.

Chapter 18

June 24, 2018

Sunday mornings. You can't beat 'em. Life seems to move at a slower pace—with the exception of those Sundays when I'm expected for lunch—and Monday morning still feels like it's nowhere in sight.

If Saturday mornings are the perfect excuse for a wank, then waking up with a gorgeous man on a Sunday is perfect for…

Yeah. I don't need to say anymore, do I?

Daniel lay beside me on his back, still sleeping, the sheet pushed down to his waist to reveal that expanse of smooth bare flesh. I gazed at his chest, wondering whether he shaved or was naturally like this. His nipples stood as proud as always, and I knew that was due to the bars through them. Then I caught movement out of the corner of my eye, and I had to smile.

Aw. How sweet. Daniel's cock is standing up to say good morning to me.

And that meant I had to look, right?

I rolled onto my side as carefully as I could, trying not to disturb him, then slowly lifted the sheet. His hard dick jerked against the cotton, and not for the first time, a thought crossed my mind.

The kind of thought that made my hole tighten and my pulse quicken.

"He's not going to get sucked if you just look at him," Daniel murmured. I jerked my head to look at his face, but his eyes were still closed.

"And what if I wasn't planning on sucking *him*?" I teased.

Daniel's eyes popped open and he let out a mock gasp. "Ssh. You'll hurt his feelings. He's sensitive."

I chuckled. "Especially after you've just come. And while sucking your dick would be a lovely way to spend the morning, I had another activity in mind. That *also* requires your dick."

Okay, I'd said it. Well, I hadn't exactly come out and said it, but I was praying he took the hint.

Daniel slowly turned his head in my direction. "Are you saying—"

"Yes," I blurted out. "Whatever it is you think I'm asking you to do, yes."

He rolled onto his side to face me. "Are you sure? There's no rule that says we have to take it in turns."

I looked him in the eye. "So you always bottom?" Hey, get me, coming out with gay sex terms. (And before you ask, yes, I *might* have done a bit more research.)

Okay, more than a bit.

Daniel blinked. “Well… no, but—”

“Oh, I get it. You don’t want to fuck me.”

He gazed at me in silence for a moment before speaking. “Firstly, I don’t think what we’ve been doing so far constitutes fucking, at least, not in *my* head. Guys talk about fucking someone, and I always picture rabbits going at it.”

Okay, that was kind of cute.

“I’m more of a *making love* man myself,” he added.

That sent a wave of warmth through me. I liked that.

“And secondly, I *do* want you. You have no idea how much. But I wasn’t about to ask.”

I swallowed. “Well… this is me asking.” I reached out and wrapped my fingers around his solid shaft, giving it a leisurely tug. “I… I want this inside me. I want to know how it feels.” Then I leaned over and kissed him, my hand still working his dick.

Daniel moaned into the kiss, his arm going around me to pull me in close. Then his hands cupped my face, holding me tenderly while we kissed.

I could kiss Daniel all day. No, seriously. If there was ever an Olympic kissing event, I think we’d win gold.

He broke the kiss and grinned. “If I’m going to put this dick where no dick has been before, I think he’s going to need all the encouragement he can get, don't you?"

I rolled my eyes. "Subtle, Daniel. Very subtle. That was Daniel-speak for 'Suck my cock', wasn't it?"

His eyes twinkled. "Wow. You speak Daniel."

As if it needed encouragement. His dick looked like it could drill through concrete. I shifted on the bed, lowering my head over his crotch and giving the head of his dick a few licks. After four or five, Daniel's hands were on my head, so I figured it was time to stop teasing and blow his mind.

I licked and sucked, flicked and teased, with tongue, lips and fingers, until he was making noise incessantly, pushing up into my mouth, his hips in constant motion. His cock isn't that fat, but it's long, and a few times he bumped the back of my throat, causing me to cough and splutter. I had visions of him sliding it into my arse so far that it reached my tonsils. And didn't *that* thought send a tremor rampaging through me?

But I wanted it too. I wanted to feel him stretch me, fill me…

As if he'd read my thoughts, Daniel pulled his dick free of my mouth. "Lie on your side, facing away from me," he said in a low voice, before grabbing the bottle of lube from the bedside table. When I did as instructed, he snuggled up behind me, his arm slipping under me so that my shoulder rested in the crook of it, his forearm across my chest, his hand on my pec. We kissed, his free hand gently working my dick, me kind of half lying on him. He eased me fully onto my side, and stroked my arse cheek, squeezing it.

My heartbeat sped up, and my throat tightened.

Daniel kissed my shoulder as he slid his fingers through my crack, unhurried and gentle. He played with my hole, rubbing his middle finger in a slow circle over it, like he'd done before. But now he pushed my knee higher toward me, opening me up to his gaze—and his fingers.

Daniel flipped open the lid of the lube bottle one-handed, and then squeezed a dribble of the clear liquid onto my hole. He put the bottle aside and kissed my shoulder again as he slowly slid his finger into my hole. My foot rested on his knee as he pushed it in deeper, and I turned my head to look at his face.

"You like it when I finger you," he said quietly.

I nodded. Since he'd introduced me to rimming, I loved it when he played with my hole. But this was different. This was getting me ready for his cock. And when he added a finger, I shivered. It burned a little, but I expected that. I knew the burn would fade.

He nodded toward the bedside table on my side. "Get me a condom?"

I grabbed one, and tore it open, before handing him the slippery latex. I watched as he rolled it down his shaft, then slicked it with more lube. Another swipe of his fingers over my hole, and then he raised his leg, bent at the knee and his foot flat to the mattress. The head of his dick pressed against my hole but didn't penetrate.

Fuck, my pounding heart…

He leaned over and kissed me, as gentle and slow as you please, his lips warm against mine as he gave a gentle push, the movement so slight as to hardly be noticeable. And still he kissed me, his hand raising my leg a little as he inched his way into my body. He grabbed my knee and pulled it toward my chest, holding onto it as he filled me, not stopping until at last he was inside me.

And then we were there, Daniel's hand on my knee, the other curled around my neck, as if he'd anchored himself to me while he lay still.

"There you go," he said, barely more than a whisper. "That's all of me." Then he kissed me, and I swear my heart was singing. When he did begin to move, it was so slowly and carefully, as if any sudden movement would shatter me into a million pieces.

"Kiss me," I begged, reaching between my legs to tug on my cock.

His lips met mine as he slid out of me, only to reverse and inch his way back into my hole, his hips rolling fluidly as he filled me then emptied me, until I was moaning into his kiss. When his cock slipped from my body, I guided it back in, wanting more, and he pushed it up inside me, rocking into me with a little more force than before.

"Yes," I groaned into his kiss. But he slowed down, moving in and out of my hole at a gentler pace, until I was crying out for him to go faster, harder, *anything* to feel him fill me to the hilt.

"It won't be long," he whispered, placing a soft kiss on my lips. "I was too close to begin with, and the way you feel on my dick…"

I moaned as he filled me to the hilt. "It's not like… it's going to be… the last time… right?"

Daniel laughed, and I felt it all the way through me. "Oh no, honey. We're going to be doing this again…" He gave a hard push, and I was as full as I could be. "And again…" Another drive of his cock into me, and I groaned. "And again…" He shuddered and gripped my knee, his other hand on my chest as he kissed me with so much passion that I was swept away by it, losing myself in a world where the only things that existed were Daniel's fingers, lips, and dick.

I tugged on my cock, my hand a blur as I neared my climax. When it came, my body tightened around Daniel's shaft, bringing a whole slew of new sensations as I shot, my body trembling against his.

He kissed my shoulder, shuddering along with me, and when I felt him throb inside me, I knew he'd finished too. He held me tightly, his breathing harsh and loud, his fingers digging into my leg as he emptied himself into the condom. Then he slid free of me, and I groaned to feel him gone.

Daniel pulled me to him, his arms around me, his lips on mine. With every kiss I wanted to hold onto this, to burn it into my memory. My heart was pounding, my skin damp with perspiration… and I had an ache where I'd never had one before.

But where I definitely wanted one again.

Daniel tilted my face to look into my eyes. "Well?"

I sighed. "Again, please?"

He laughed. "What—right now?"

I pretended to consider the question carefully. "Maybe not," I said at last. When he chuckled, I added, "Give me half an hour."

He kissed me, one of those slow and easy kisses that left me wanting more. "There *is* something I'd like you to consider."

"Oh?"

"Well… every three months, come rain or shine, I get tested. For STIs, HIV, you name it. And even if I haven't been with anyone in months, I still do it, because it's a good habit to get into."

"What kind of test are we talking?"

"A little prick, that's all."

I glanced down at his crotch. "Aw, don't call him that. You'll give him an inferiority complex." I smirked. When Daniel sighed, I traced the line of his softening dick with my finger. The latex still clung to it. "I would *never* call your cock inferior, trust me. Not after feeling the aftereffects of it."

"Will you think about it?"

I knew where he was going, of course. "So… I get tested… and we ditch the condoms. Is that the idea?" Not that I'd ever had sex without one. I liked being careful.

He nodded. "And for the record… I've always used condoms in the past."

But he didn't want to use them with me. The full force of what Daniel was suggesting struck home.

He wants commitment.

It wasn't like he'd asked me to marry him, right?

But it's as good as. He doesn't want an open relationship. He doesn't want to have sex with anyone else. Just me.

"And then… we could go together to get tested."

I met his gaze. "As a couple." He nodded.

Okay, things had just got serious.

"I'll look into it," I said in a firm voice.

I could tell by his expression that he'd

hoped for a more unequivocal, enthusiastic answer, but his request had taken me by surprise, and I needed time to think. If I did this, it would be for the right reasons.

And what are *the right reasons?*

As if I knew. But he asked me to think about it, right? So… I was going to do just that. He didn't have to know I wasn't that fond of needles, did he?

Then I reasoned that if I could overcome that fear for anyone, it would be for him.

I kissed him on the mouth, letting my lips linger there. When we parted, I glanced down at our bodies. "I think a shower is called for, don't you?"

"That depends." He smiled. "Will you be in there with me?"

"Of course. Health and Safety, remember?" He laughed at that. "Then what?"

"I was thinking breakfast, then…" His eyes sparkled. "How about we finish watching the rest of the Lord of the Rings trilogy?"

"Only if we get to watch them in here."

Daniel laughed. "Why do I think it's going to be another naked day?"

I kissed the tip of his nose. "Because they're the best kind." I waited until he'd left the room and was heading for the bathroom, before sagging against the pillows.

This was new.

This was also a little scary.

Could I see myself going to the nearest clinic for a test?

I had a feeling I already knew the answer to that.

Chapter 19

Wednesday June 27, 2018

I walked from the station, my phone against my ear. "I missed you." I liked traveling home with Daniel, and I'd be happy when Pride was over, and all his rehearsals were over too.

"You'll see me Saturday. I'm just thankful Mac keeps his weekend rehearsals to Sundays only."

"Then you're still coming?" I still hadn't worked out what I was going to say to the guys. I wasn't going to let Daniel simply turn up on the doorstep and bring him in. Although… the look on Justin's face would be entertaining.

"Of course." He paused. "Are you nervous about telling them?"

"A little. Well, strictly speaking, there's only Justin and Moz to tell." I wanted them to like Daniel, because if I had my way, he'd be spending a lot of weekends at the house.

The noise in the background increased. "Where are you?"

"At McDonalds, grabbing a bite before rehearsal. A load of teenagers just came in." Daniel sighed. "I'd better go. I'll call you tonight as usual?"

"I'll be waiting," I assured him.

"I woke up thinking of you this morning," he said, lowering his voice.

"Nice thoughts, I hope?"

He chuckled. "Hot thoughts, actually."

"Ooh, my favourite kind. Keep those in mind for when you call tonight."

"I can see how *that* call is going to go." He laughed. "You always sleep better after you've come."

"Then be prepared to give me a good night's sleep," I said before disconnecting. My heart felt light, and despite being the end of a long day, I had a spring in my step. I was already looking forward to his call, and it had nothing to do with the prospect of getting off with him.

It was more to do with hearing his voice.

As I reached my front door, my phone buzzed again. This time it was Rachel.

Instantly my heartbeat rocketed. "Are you okay? Is everything all right with the baby?"

She chuckled. "Calm down. I'm fine. I'm calling to see how things are going."

"By 'things', you mean Daniel." I opened the door and let myself in. Inside the house was quiet as usual.

"Of course. You're still seeing him?"

A warm glow stole through me. "Oh yeah."

I walked into the kitchen, dropped my bag on the work top, and filled the kettle, my phone wedged between my shoulder and ear. "In fact, we're having a barbecue here on Saturday, and he's coming."

"Wow. You're coming out to your housemates?"

"It's not that big a deal," I protested. "Half of them already know." But still my heartbeat raced at the thought. It *was* a big deal.

"I still think it's great."

I knew I had something else to tell her. "I'm going to Pride, by the way," I said as I spooned coffee into a mug.

"Oh, I'm glad," she said warmly. "Good for you. I'll look out for you on the evening news when they show video of the parade, so make sure you stand out from the crowd."

I snorted. "Oh, I don't think so." When she went quiet, I knew something was up. "Rach?"

"How long have you two been together now?"

I did a swift mental calculation. "Three weeks." Three wonderful weeks that had changed my life for the better.

"And are there signs that it's going to last?"

How the hell could I answer that? How do any of us know how long a relationship will last? Nothing is fixed, right? "I think so. I *hope* so."

Yeah. My head might not have been sure,

but my heart was.

"Then maybe it's time to think about telling Mum and Dad you have a boyfriend?"

Oh God.

Telling Justin and Moz was one thing—telling my parents was another thing entirely.

"If you want me there for moral support, you only have to ask. You know that, don't you?"

I sighed. She was right, of course. "I need to talk to Daniel about this."

"Of course you do. And Lee? I can't wait to meet him."

That made me smile. "You'll love him."

"I think it's more important that you do," she said quietly before saying goodbye and disconnecting.

I stared at the kettle, not really seeing it. With one calmly uttered statement, she'd brought my world to a grinding halt.

Do I love him?

I leaned against the work top, my head in a spin. *How do I know if what I'm feeling is love?* I had nothing to go on, no previous relationships where I'd been head-over heels. *Am I* capable *of falling head-over-heels for someone?*

"Er, Lee? The kettle's boiled."

I jerked my head toward the doorway where Mick stood, his laptop in his hands, watching me with an amused expression.

"Oh. Yeah. Right." I poured water into the

mug.

Mick came into the kitchen and put the laptop down on the work top. "Are you okay?"

"Sure," I replied, more lightly than I felt. Mick stared at me, and I sighed heavily. "No, I'm not. My sister just said something that got me thinking, but it's nothing you can help me with. This one, I have to deal with on my own." But there *was* something I'd meant to share with him. "I've invited Daniel to the barbecue. He's staying here this weekend."

Mick's eyes widened. "Wow. Okay." He smiled. "I guess it's serious then?"

To my way of thinking, standing in the kitchen, debating whether I was in love with Daniel counted as serious. The logical part of my brain was shouting that it had only been *three bloody weeks*. That people didn't fall in love after three weeks of knowing someone.

Except I knew that was bullshit. Rachel had known, right? So had my gran.

I peered at Mick. "Do you love Pete?" I asked abruptly.

He blinked. "I'm not sure that's any of your business, but yes, I love him."

"When did you know you loved him? I mean, the moment you realized?"

Mick reached into the cabinet, removed a mug, and reboiled the kettle. "If I'm honest? About two weeks after that fateful weekend where we ended up in bed together. We'd talked every night of those two weeks. I couldn't go to sleep until we'd spoken on the phone." He smiled. "I remember the first time I told him I loved him. We were both in bed, on Face Time. One of those sleepy conversations where neither of us wanted to say goodnight. When he said it was time, I blurted out those three little words." Mick chuckled. "Suddenly he was very much awake. He said he'd been dying to say something all week, but hadn't dared." He rubbed his hand over his shaved head. "What can I say? The rest is history."

"Can you see yourselves continuing a long-distance relationship?"

Mick bit his lip. "I've been thinking about this a lot lately."

I got the feeling I wasn't the only one with decisions to make.

As Mick made himself a coffee, an idea occurred. "You know they say there's safety in numbers, right?"

Mick gave me an inquiring glance. "What are you thinking of?"

"Well… if I'm bringing Daniel to the barbecue… you could bring Pete."

He stilled. "You're serious." I nodded, and Mick chuckled. "Talk about ripping off a Band-aid." He rubbed his chin thoughtfully. "You've got a point though. If we both bring boyfriends… I'll have to talk to Pete about it."

"You do that. But I'd do it quickly. When does he arrive?"

"He's on the 6.55 train Saturday morning. He gets into Kings Cross just before midday. I'm going to collect him. I *was* going to take him straight to his hotel…"

"Talk to him. Decide what you want to do." I smiled. "It's okay if you don't want to tell them."

He sighed. "Yeah, but right now I'm thinking the positives outweigh the negatives. No more hiding. I like that idea." He stared into his mug, apparently lost in his thoughts.

I nudged him. "Milk, Mick."

He frowned. "Hm?"

I pointed to his coffee. "Milk. You don't drink it black." We were as bad as each other. Both of us, distracted by our men.

I couldn't think of anything better to be distracted by.

#lovewins
love is love

"This is nice." Daniel lay on his side facing the camera, his arm curled under his pillow. His upper body was bare, and I couldn't see the sheet that covered the rest of him. If there was a sheet.

I mirrored his position, my phone propped

up against a pillow. "I wanted to see you."

Daniel let out a happy sigh. "No complaints here."

"How was rehearsal?"

He shrugged his shoulder. "Okay. Mac thinks we're ready. We should be, the amount of work we've put into this." He chuckled. "Even David has finally got his act together and perfected his Dirty Dancing lift."

I couldn't wait to see that.

"There's a possibility we might not be the only same-sex couple at the barbecue."

Daniel widened his eyes. "Really? Who else is coming?"

I wasn't going to say more, not until Mick came to a decision. "Wait and see. It might not happen." I paused. "My sister can't wait to meet you."

His face glowed. "Aw, that's nice."

"She suggested it might be a good time to tell my parents."

Daniel became very still. "And what do *you* think about that?"

"Hey, you're in this too, remember? Because if—when—I tell them, I won't be there on my own. I'd want you with me." I wasn't going to even *contemplate* doing this without him.

Daniel regarded me with a calm expression. "If you want me there, I'll be there. Whenever you decide you're ready."

The way he looked at me, the quiet confidence in his voice…

"This is serious, isn't it?" When he frowned, I took a deep breath. "Us, I mean." My heart pounded.

Daniel's lips parted and a soft sigh escaped them. Finally, he nodded. "*I* think so."

His self-assured response eased the tightness around my chest. "I think so too." I let out a shaky laugh.

"What's funny?" Daniel propped himself up, his weight on his elbow, his head resting in his hand.

"This. All of it. It's so… new. Scary. Exciting. All of the above."

Daniel laughed quietly. "Great, isn't it?"

Oh God, it really was.

I came to a decision. "If you're staying here Saturday night, then how about on Sunday, I take you to meet them? I'll tell Mum I'm bringing a guest, because she'll want us to stay for lunch."

Daniel bit his lip. "Sunday lunch with the boyfriend's parents. Wow. This *is* serious." His eyes twinkled in the lamplight. "What's her cooking like?"

I sighed. "I don't think MasterChef will be calling her anytime soon."

"Gotcha." Daniel stared at me. "You look good in that light."

I smiled. "You look good in any light."

Then I noticed the slight movement of his upper arm. “What are you doing?”

“Looking at you and remembering.”

A wave of heat surged through me. “Remembering what?” As if I didn’t know.

“You here beside me, while I slowly filled you again and again.” There was definite movement now, and I knew exactly what was happening off-screen.

I reached for the bottle of lube on the bedside table, slicked up my fingers, and curled them around my stiffening dick. I didn’t say a word. Neither of us did after that, but we made plenty of sounds, soft sighs, low moans, the odd gasp of pleasure… In my head I was there in his bed, Sunday morning, Daniel inside me, and it was so good, so sensual.

It should have felt weird, the pair of us staring at each other on our phones as we brought ourselves to orgasm, my gaze locked on his parted lips, his heaving chest, those gorgeous eyes that looked into mine…

It wasn’t long before both of us were breathing faster, and our low cries were almost in sync when I came, creaming my hand, thinking of him, hearing him, smelling him…I grabbed a tissue and cleaned up, while he did the same.

I stared at the screen. “Sweet dreams, Daniel.”

His sated smile was beautiful. “Sweet

dreams, Lee."

#LoveWins
love is love

Friday June 28, 2018

"The pizzas are here!" I yelled up the stairs. Within seconds came the thud of feet as Justin, Moz and Niall thundered down the staircase. Mick had already placed the boxes on the table, and I removed plates from the cabinet. Glasses full of ice stood on the worktop, ready for the Coke.

Justin yanked open one of the pizza boxes and sniffed up. "Can't beat that smell."

Moz laughed. "You say the same thing every Friday."

"He eats the same *pizza* every Friday," Mick commented. "Ever think of changing things up a little, Justin?"

He snorted. "I asked for olives this time instead of anchovies. That's a change, isn't it? What more do you want?"

"You know what they say," Niall said with a twinkle in his eye. "Variety is the spice of life, and all that."

I glanced at Mick. I wasn't going to get a better opening than that.

"Speaking of variety…" I took a mouthful

of Coke before continuing. “I’m bringing someone special to the barbecue tomorrow.” I was doing my damnedest to maintain a calm front, but my heart was racing.

Justin grinned. “I knew it. There’s been something about you these last few weeks. All this sneaking off at the weekends, not telling anyone where you’re going…” He gave a smug smile. “Lee’s-got-a-girl-friend,” he sang.

“*Almost* right.” When he stared at me, I smiled. “Lee’s-got-a-boy-friend.” There. Said it. Well… sang it.

Justin’s jaw dropped and his eyes widened. Then he gave Moz a triumphant glance. “Pay up. You lose.” Moz grumbled and pulled his wallet from his back pocket.

“What?” I gaped at them.

Moz shook his head. “He said the reason you weren’t telling us anything was because you’d turned gay.” He slapped a ten-pound note into Justin’s palm.

“Then strictly speaking, Justin lost.” I gave them both a sweet smile. “I’m not gay, I’m bi.”

“Ha!” Moz snatched it back and reinserted it into his wallet.

Mick and Niall were laughing their arses off. I was still reeling from the fact that Justin had guessed.

Justin peered at them suspiciously. “You knew, didn’t you?”

Niall preened. “Yup.”

My heartbeat was returning to normal. *That wasn’t so bad, was it?*

“Well, I’m glad you told us tonight.” Justin’s eyes sparkled. “I wouldn’t want to embarrass myself tomorrow by saying something stupid when he gets here.”

“I wouldn’t worry about that,” I remarked. “I’d bet money on you coming out with *some* stupid comment before the barbecue is over.” Justin narrowed his gaze briefly, but the others were laughing.

“So what’s his name?” Moz asked.

“Daniel.”

“And mine’s called Pete,” Mick said suddenly before taking a long drink from his glass.

Three jaws dropped.

“Your what?” Justin asked at last.

“My boyfriend,” Mick said in a matter-of-fact tone that impressed the hell out of me. “In fact, he’ll be staying the weekend.”

I patted Mick on the back. “I can’t wait to meet him,” I said sincerely.

Moz blinked, his pizza forgotten. Niall was smiling and shaking his head.

Justin dropped his slice of pizza onto his plate. “Christ, it’s like buses. There’s never one around when you need one, and then two come at once.” He cleared his throat. “So how long has all this been going on?”

"Three weeks for me," I said, helping myself to another slice of Hawaiian.

"Three years for me," Mick added.

"Three ye—" Justin's mouth fell open again.

Mick glanced at me and chuckled. "I think we just broke Justin."

I snickered. "Trust me. He won't stay broken for long." I felt brilliant.

This really is going to be okay.

That only left my parents. And I couldn't see *them* taking the news as easily as Justin and Moz had.

Chapter 20

Saturday June 30, 2018

"Isn't there something you should be doing?" Daniel asked with a grin. He sat astride me on my bed, where we'd been ever since he arrived half an hour before. The kitchen had been a hive of activity, but I'd already done my bit. I'd been up since eight, slicing burger buns and hot dog rolls, making sure the house was spotless, and mowing the grass. As soon as Daniel came through the front door, I whisked him upstairs.

He'd meet everyone soon enough.

"The only important thing I need to be doing right now is kissing you," I told him. "I have a week's worth of kisses to catch up on."

"Sounds good to me," he said with a sigh, before leaning down to claim my lips in a long, sensual kiss. "Missed you."

I curved my hand around his nape. "Missed you too." Then I slid my hands down his back until I reached his arse. I gently squeezed his cheeks. "Have I told you how much I like these shorts?"

Daniel snorted. "You just like my arse."

"And your point is?" I squeezed again. "It's a very nice arse. It's touchable. Biteable. Lickable."

I leaned in closer. "Fuckable."

Daniel pressed his palms against my chest. "Down, boy. We are *not* getting up to anything before tonight. You've got a barbecue to host, remember?"

I brought my hand to his crotch. "Seems to me something has already got up." His dick pressed against the zipper of his denim shorts.

He nuzzled my neck, and I shivered as I always did. "All I have to do is look at you and he stands to attention," Daniel whispered.

"Then maybe I'd better take him out and pay him some attention," I suggested with a grin. I licked my lips and it was Daniel's turn to shiver.

"I've been dreaming all week about your mouth on my cock," he admitted, his eyes shining.

I popped the button on his waistband, grasped the zipper, and—

"Where's Mick?" Justin hollered from downstairs. "We need him."

I froze. "That doesn't sound good."

Daniel was off me in a flash. "Then let's go see what the problem is." He gave me a frank stare. "You can't keep me up here all day. I'll have to meet them eventually." He redid the button on his shorts.

He was right, of course. "Come on then."

He followed me out of the room and down the stairs to where Justin was standing, his short hair spikier than ever where he'd obviously been running his hands through it. His eyes widened when he caught sight of Daniel, but then he snapped his attention to me.

"Where's Mick?"

"He's gone into London to meet Pete's train. What's the problem?"

Justin glared at me. "The problem? Oh, not much of one. I can't get the fucking barbecue to light, that's all, and everyone will be arriving soon." He gave Daniel an apologetic glance. "Sorry about that. Hello. You're Daniel. I'm Justin. And I'm a bit stressed right now."

"No shit," I muttered.

Daniel smacked me on the arm, then focused on Justin. "What kind of barbecue is it?"

Justin blinked. "It's a barbecue."

"Yes, but is it gas or charcoal?" Daniel asked patiently.

He blinked. "Oh. Oh yeah. It's charcoal. A kettle thingy."

"And have you got the vents open?"

Justin blinked again. "It has vents?"

Daniel chuckled. "Lead me to the barbecue. I'll soon have it going."

Justin heaved a huge sigh of relief. "Oh, thank God. Someone who's knows what he's doing." He led Daniel through the kitchen and into the garden, me trailing after them. The kettle barbecue sat on the patio. "I lit the coals, but they won't stay lit."

Daniel peered into the kettle, frowning. "But… you've only got a few charcoal briquettes in here. That's not enough."

Justin groaned. "Look, I don't know how to light a real barbecue, okay? That was supposed to be Mick's job. Only, he's gone off to pick up the boyfriend we never even knew existed until last night. I've only ever dealt with throwaway barbecues, and they're easy as piss to light."

Daniel laid a hand on Justin's arm. "It's okay. And just so you know what to do in the future, here's How To Light A Barbecue For Dummies." His lips twitched.

Justin stared at him for a moment, then chuckled. "I think you're gonna fit right in around here." He gestured to the kettle. "Go for it."

Daniel pointed to the vents on the hood. "These control the flow of air to the coals. Once the coals are lit, keep them open. It'll get the barbecue going quicker. You can shut them again once the coals are ready to cook over. And you don't need to cover the whole of the base with coals."

"Why not?"

"If you heap your coals in the middle, that means you can use the other parts of the rack to warm food on. In general, a thinner, taller pile of charcoal goes up in flames better than a thin widely spread layer. Once the coals are burning through and turning white, you can spread them out a bit." Daniel lifted the wire rack and piled charcoal briquettes in the centre. Then he placed firelighters around them and used a match to light them. "Okay, now we open the vents. You should leave that to burn for about twenty to thirty minutes. Then you can spread them out." Daniel straightened.

Justin was beaming. "Thank you. Looks like we didn't need Mick after all." He inclined his head toward the back door. "Moz has made some punch, if you'd like a glass."

Daniel cocked his head to one side. "Is it alcoholic?"

"Er, yeah."

Daniel grinned. "Thank God. Then yes, I'll have a glass." He glanced at me. "And so will you."

Justin chuckled. "Oh yeah. You'll *really* fit right in around here." He peered at me. "He's all right, your fella." Then he went into the house to fetch the punch.

Daniel waited until he was out of sight before turning to me. "Well? How did I do?"

"Justin's not the only one who's impressed. How come you know so much about barbecues?"

Daniel's face tightened. "Trying growing up around my dad and *not* knowing how to light one. He trained me from an early age."

"He did a great job then," I said softly, before leaning in and kissing him on the mouth.

"Oops. Shall I come back later?" Justin

stood there with two glasses of punch, in which floated pieces of apple and orange. He handed them to us. "So how did you two meet?" He inclined his head toward me. "Because this one's told us bugger all about you."

"There'll be time for small talk later," I said quickly. "Let's make sure everything's ready first."

"Okay, okay, don't get your lacy knickers in a twist," Justin said good-naturedly. Then he sprinted back into the house, chuckling.

Daniel arched his eyebrows. "'Lacy knickers'?"

I held up my hands. "Hey, don't look at me. I never breathed a word."

"I see. Then it's a case of 'I'm gay therefore I wear lacy knickers.'" He snorted.

"Yeah, but he was talking to *me* when he said it, and *I* don't wear them." I leaned in close and whispered, "But are you?"

Daniel's eyes gleamed. "Of course."

I had a feeling the barbecue was going to be more fun than I'd anticipated.

#lovewins

love is love

By two in the afternoon, the little back garden was full to bursting: there had to be around twenty-five people crammed in there. Guests sat on the patio chairs, on every chair we'd dragged out of the house, or on the grass. Niall had set up his iPod with its speakers, and music drifted from the house, pleasant and not obtrusive.

The food had gone down well, and Mick had been in charge of grilling, so thankfully nothing had been cremated. Pete was a quiet kind of guy, and he spent most of the time sitting beside Mick, watching the proceedings and chatting with Mick or Daniel.

"Anyone want to play on the PlayStation?" Moz asked, and several guests got up and went into the house to join him. Justin had done a good job of mingling, making sure everyone had enough food or drink. By two o'clock we figured people would help themselves if they wanted anything. Right then he was occupied with Valerie, a girl who worked at the same gym.

When Norah Jones's *Come Away With Me* came on, Daniel nudged my arm. "Dance with me?"

I stared at him for a second, the question not sinking in. Then I saw he was serious. "Here?"

He gestured to the patio, which was empty. "Why not? While we have the space?"

Fuck it.

I got to my feet. "Okay."

Daniel beamed, took me by the hand, and led me to the little patio. He put his hands on my waist, I looped my arms around his neck, and we moved to the slow, sweet music.

I expelled a breath. "Okay, I didn't see this coming."

Daniel pressed his cheek against mine. "There's nothing wrong with a little slow dancing. Now, if it changes to *rap*, I'm outta here."

I laughed, enjoying the feel of his hands on me. Then I realized we were no longer alone—Mick and Pete were dancing too. I glanced at them, but Mick appeared lost in his own world, his gaze focused on the man in his arms.

"Well, if *they're* dancing…" a voice announced from the far side of the garden. Seconds later, Valerie had tugged Justin across the grass to the patio. Then they too were moving to the music.

"We seem to have started something," Daniel murmured. "They look like they're having fun."

"They? They who?" I looked him in the eye. "All I can see is you."

Daniel's eyes glistened. "Remind me to thank you for that later, when we're alone." His cheek was once more against mine, and I breathed in his familiar scent.

I couldn't wait until we were alone.

#LoveWins
love is love

About half the guests had gone by six, but Moz had had the idea of doing Karaoke, and so we piled into the larger of the two lounges. Moz had the lyrics up on the TV screen, and guests chose their songs.

I had to admit, it was a lot of fun, even if one or two of the guests' singing sounded like someone was strangling a cat. We applauded politely all the same. The songs were more varied than I'd expected. Frank Sinatra was in there, as was Elton John, Queen, the Stones, along with Adele and Ed Sheeran.

"My turn," Daniel said quietly before getting up off the couch and walking over to Moz to peer at his list of karaoke tracks.

Mick nudged me. "Can he sing?" he asked in a quiet voice.

"I have no idea." I sat with bated breath, awaiting those first few notes.

When the words flashed up on the screen, I frowned. "Have you heard of this one? I think it's way before my time." I'd never heard of Roberta Flack.

Mick caught his breath. "Oh wow."

Before I could question his reaction, Daniel

sang the first line, and it was about seeing a face for the first time.

Holy fucking crap, Daniel could really *sing*.

Then I forgot my amazement and listened to the lyrics. It had to be one of the most beautiful—and intimate—songs I'd ever heard, and it was obvious from the first note that he was singing it to me, because he never once looked at the TV screen, only at me. I sat there, my heart racing, as he sang of kissing me and feeling the earth move. He sang of lying with me, our hearts close together, and although I knew the words weren't his, he *made* them his. And when he sang of a joy that would last till the end of time, I wanted to cry. Because in that moment, Daniel was laying bare his soul and telling everyone in that room how he felt—about me.

When he was done, Daniel locked his eyes on mine, and I put my hand to my chest, as if to still my beating heart. Applause echoed around the room, dying away as the next guest got up to sing. I waited for Daniel to re-join me on the couch, my heart still pounding, but it seemed he had other ideas.

"Excuse me." Daniel left the room in a hurry.

"Well fuck," Justin murmured. I glanced at him, torn between staying because we had guests, and following Daniel.

"What's the matter?" I asked.

Justin sighed. "I reckon you've got the right idea, changing teams. I've never had a girl look at me the way Daniel looked at you."

"And how was that?" I was still shaken by the lyrics, the way he'd stared directly at me as he'd sung them.

The emotion in those expressive eyes…

Justin gazed at me frankly. "Like you're the best thing since sliced bread. Now go after him. We can manage here."

I didn't hesitate. I dashed from the room and went into the kitchen. No Daniel. I headed up the stairs to my room, but when I entered the room, I came to a thudding halt.

Daniel was sitting on my bed, his head in his hands.

I went over to him and knelt in front of him. "What's wrong?" My stomach churned.

He looked at me, taking my face in both hands. "I'm sorry. I… I got carried away down there."

"Don't you dare apologize." I grabbed his head and pulled him in for a kiss that I hoped would show him how deeply he'd moved me. Daniel enfolded me in his arms, and the kiss deepened.

When it broke, I looked him in the eye. "What you sang… It was beautiful."

Daniel didn't break eye contact. "I meant it. Every word."

I couldn't deny what my heart was telling me a moment longer. "I love you. I don't care how long we've known each—"

He stopped my words with a kiss, and I fucking *melted*. I locked my arms around him and held on as he lifted me to my feet, his arms wrapped around me, holding me against his body.

"I love you too." He smiled. "And I will do until the end of time….my love.'"

Those had been the lyrics that had stolen the breath from me.

I stroked his cheek. "Make love to me?"

His breathing hitched. "God, yes."

Then I bolted my door, drew the curtains, and undressed him, like we had all the time in the world.

Chapter 21

Sunday July 1, 2018

The first thing I noticed when I opened my eyes was that Daniel wasn't there.

Actually, I knew that with my eyes closed. It's like sleeping with a hot water bottle with him in the bed. And that's not a complaint, especially when bits of him are both warm *and* hard.

The door opened, and he crept back into the room, wearing just his shorts. I glanced at the alarm clock: it was still early. Daniel climbed back into bed, and I held my arms wide in invitation. He cuddled up to me, and I pulled the sheet over us.

This was… bliss.

Then I corrected myself. Bliss would be *without* the shorts.

Thankfully, he seemed to realize that at the same moment. He reached beneath the sheet and wriggled out of them before tossing them onto the floor. Then his head was on my shoulder, and we were kissing, slow *well hello there* kisses, as if we were learning the feel, taste and smell of each other all over again.

Daniel stroked down my chest and belly, until his fingertips brushed over the head of my very interested dick. He grinned.

I shook my head. “No. No way. They’ll hear.”

Daniel stared at me. “What about last night? Neither of us was exactly quiet.” He bit back a smile.

“Yeah, but there was karaoke going on downstairs. A herd of elephants could’ve stampeded through here, and no one would’ve noticed.”

He chuckled. “Seems like Justin has no qualms about making a noise.”

I rolled my eyes. “Oh, it’s wank time again, is it? Trust me, we’ve all heard him.”

Daniel rolled on top of me, his forearms bracketing my head. “Yeah, but he’s not alone… unless he’s perfecting his ventriloquism act and is throwing a female voice.” He chuckled again.

I blinked. “Oh.” Then I narrowed my gaze. “Exactly what is the female voice saying?”

Danie’s voice went higher. “Oh, Justin, you’re so big.”

I snickered. “Then yeah, he might be doing voices. I wouldn’t put it past him anyway.”

Daniel grinned again, reaching between us to grasp my cock. “So…”

“No,” I said firmly. “This is not a competition. ‘He’s doing it so we can too.’ Besides…” I pulled him up toward me and kissed him softly on the lips. “I wanted to snuggle with you."

It was as if someone flicked a switch, and Horny Daniel morphed into Sweet Daniel, who kissed me like I was something precious and fragile.

"I didn't dream last night, did I?" I asked in a low voice between kisses.

Daniel stroked my cheek. "Which part? The bit where I declared my feelings for you in a startlingly intimate song in front of your guests?"

I smiled. "I was thinking about the bit when you said you loved me."

His face glowed. "And then you said you loved me too. And you certainly didn't dream what came next."

If it had been a dream, it was one I would never forget.

I'd asked him to make love to me, and he'd done just that. Every touch of his hands, every kiss, every stroke of his dick inside me… And when I came, it had been to the sound of Daniel telling me again that he loved me.

"I was going to ask you something last night, but I guess I got carried away."

I wound my fingers through his hair where it was longer on top. "Then ask me now."

"Did you find time this last week to go get a little prick?"

I coughed. "Would you mind rephrasing that?" Not that I didn't know what he was referring to.

He laughed. "Did you go and get tested? I know it was only a suggestion, but…"

I nodded, my heartbeat climbing a little. "I am germ-free, bug-free…" I didn't tell him how long it had taken me to get up enough nerve to walk into the clinic. And the thought that I would have to do it again every three months?

It's a good thing I love him, right?

Daniel's slow smile made something in my belly uncoil, sending heat radiating through me. "I am *so* glad to hear that." He sat up, lifting one leg gracefully to straddle me. Then he leaned forward to grab the bottle of lube from where we'd left it the previous night. After squeezing some into his palm, he reached behind him and curled his fingers around my hard dick, slicking it from root to tip.

I caught my breath, anticipating the first time I would feel his body wrapped around my bare cock.

Daniel nodded, his gaze locked on mine as he shifted back a little. "I'll be quiet."

I grinned. "No, you won't. It's not in your vocabulary when it comes to sex." I stroked his belly. "They can all be jealous as fuck for all I care." Then I gasped as he eased the head into him. Daniel sank down slowly, until at last all of me was inside him.

The *heat* of him…

He sighed happily. "I love a good ride first

thing in the morning."

My hands were on his hips, lifting him, then pulling him down onto my shaft. "I see what you mean. I may take it up myself."

The door was shut, the house was quiet, and I was making love to Daniel, with no barriers between us.

Yeah. *This* was bliss.

#LoveWins
love is love

"Will I do?" Daniel asked as we approached the front door.

I smiled. "You look adorable." He'd decided to leave off the makeup, which hadn't surprised me. He was trying to make this go as smoothly as possible, and him walking in with his usual lip gloss, eye liner and eye shadow was not the way to do that.

"Let them get used to the idea of me first," he'd said as we were getting ready. "I don't want to be responsible for giving your mum a heart attack the first time she meets me."

I'd laughed. "I think she's seen guys wearing makeup before."

"Sure, but not on a guy who's dating her son."

He had a point.

I took a deep breath and rang the doorbell. A minute later, Mum opened it, smiling when she saw me. She gave Daniel a polite nod, before standing aside to let us into the hall.

"I'll be honest, I was a bit surprised when you said you were coming for lunch," she said. "I mean, you were only here two weeks ago." Daniel got an inquiring glance.

"This is Daniel, Mum."

Daniel held out his hand. "It's a pleasure to meet you, Mrs. Tennant."

She shook it, then waved dismissively. "Please, call me Molly. Mrs. Tennant was what I called my mother-in-law." She gave him another quizzical glance, and I could almost hear the cogs clicking and whirring in her head.

Well, explanations would have to wait.

"Where's Dad?" As if I had to ask: the sound of roaring football fans came from the TV in the living room.

"Go on in. I'll bring us some tea." She gave a half smile. "I didn't expect you for another hour at least. You're not usually this early."

"That would be my fault, Mrs—Molly," Daniel said apologetically. "I hate being late."

That got him a look of approval. "Well, if this is the influence you're having on Lee, you're welcome to come to Sunday lunch again." She ushered us into the living room, where Dad was sprawled in his armchair, wearing his favourite worn plaid slippers that always reminded me of Wallace from the Wallace and Gromit films.

He glanced up as we came into the room, and straightened hurriedly after switching off the TV with the remote. "Oh. I didn't expect you yet." He got to his feet, his hand extended to Daniel. "And you are?"

"Daniel Bond, Mr. Tennant."

Dad's eyes twinkled as they shook hands. "Any relation to James?"

Daniel gave a laugh that sounded like he'd never heard anyone make that joke before. "I'm afraid not."

Dad gestured to the couch. "Well. Sit down then." He fired me a glance. "Where's your mum?"

"Fetching tea," I told him.

He chuckled. "Of course." He retook his seat in the armchair. "So, Daniel… you're a friend of Lee's?"

"That's right," Daniel replied with a polite smile.

(Well, he *is* my friend. My *boy*friend.)

Dad laced his fingers together, his elbows resting on the chair arms. "Well, you're the first friend he'd ever brought here for lunch. I suppose we'll find out why that is in a minute?" He looked to me for confirmation.

Yeah, my dad's not stupid.

Mum bustled in with a tray, on which sat

the fat brown teapot that had been around since I was a kid, and four china mugs, plus a sugar bowl and milk jug. She set the tray down on the table next to my dad's chair and proceeded to pour.

"So, Daniel," Mum said in a cheerful voice, "How do you know our Lee?"

Daniel gave me a *What do I say now?* look, and I knew it was time to bite the bullet. "Actually, Mum, Dad…. Daniel's my boyfriend."

A spoon clattered into the sugar bowl, and Mum made a strangled noise as if she'd just swallowed a frog. Dad stared at us, blinked, blinked again, and then got up out of his chair and walked to the bay window, his back to us.

"Well, that went down well," I remarked in a bright voice.

Dad whirled around and strode over to us. He opened and closed his mouth a couple of times, then finally he sank heavily back into his armchair. "Well, at least that explains why Ben was so… off with me the other Sunday."

"Oh, Ben wasn't saying those things because of me," I explained. "In fact, he had no idea about me at that time. He was talking about his younger brother, Gary, who's gay."

"Ben's brother is gay?" That frog was still in Mum's throat from the sound of it.

I nodded cheerfully.

"Bloody hell." Dad stared at us. "They're coming out of the woodwork."

"Ah." I took a breath. "I think this is the point where I tell you I'm *not* gay."

Dad blinked. "You could've fooled me." He jerked his head toward Daniel. "So what's he then? Chopped liver?"

"He's still my boyfriend, but I'm bisexual." I sighed. "I know I'm throwing a lot at you, but I wanted you to know." I gazed at my dad with concern. "Are we okay?"

Dad frowned. "Of course we're okay. I'm just confused as fu—"

"Geoff," Mum said in a warning tone of voice.

Dad cleared his throat. "So… what was Cheryl then?"

"She was my girlfriend at the time."

Dad huffed. "First you've got a girlfriend. Then you've got a boyfriend. Is this it now? Have you made up your mind?"

I bit back a smile. "It doesn't work like that, Dad."

"Well, are you going to change your mind further down the road?"

"It doesn't work that way either." I glanced at Daniel, who I knew was staying out of it until he had something to say. I let out a patient sigh. "I'm interested in both men *and* women. That doesn't mean I'm going to go out with every man and woman that I come across, okay? There's just Daniel. I mean, *you're* into women, but you don't date every woman you meet, right?" I gave Dad a sympathetic glance. "I know it's been a bit of a shock, but—"

"A bit?" Dad's eyes were like saucers.

"Okay, a big shock then."

Daniel laid his hand on my arm, then addressed my mum. "You *can* ask questions, you know."

Mum bit her lip. "I… I don't know what to say to you. I'm afraid of offending you, or hurting your feelings."

Daniel gave her a warm smile. "If you're asking questions from a genuine desire to understand, then there are no questions that are off the table, okay? If a question's not coming from a bad place, then it's fine."

I gazed at him, pride swelling in my chest. (*This* is why I love Daniel. He's got a warm heart and he knows exactly what to say.)

Mum shook her head. "I didn't know what to say to your uncle Charlie either, when he first told me he was into fellas."

It was my turn to blink. "Uncle Charlie is gay?"

Dad snorted. "You mean you didn't know?"

"Er… no?" (I have a gay uncle? Why didn't anybody tell me this?)

Okay, maybe this is the point where I add I haven't seen Uncle Charlie since I was seven, which is when he emigrated to Australia.

Mum's eyes lit up. "Ooh. Do you think it might be useful if you talked to him? He might be able to give you a few pointers."

I was doing my best not to laugh my arse off at this point.

"I think I'm fine, Mum," I said, with more calm that I felt. "Besides… there's the whole *I'm not gay, I'm bi* thing, remember?"

She nodded. "Sorry. I keep forgetting." She held a china mug out to Daniel. "Tea?"

He took it, and I could see his lips were twitching too.

Okay, this really hadn't gone the way I'd expected, but you know what? It was a start. Baby steps, Daniel had said that morning, and he was right, of course. Who knew where we'd be a year from now?

I knew where *I* wanted to be.

Still in love with Daniel.

#lovewins

love is love

Mum waved at us as we shut the front gate behind us, then closed the front door. I shuddered out a breath. "Wow."

"Good wow or bad wow?"

"I think it was an 'I can't believe that just

happened' wow." Maybe Rachel had them nailed the whole time. Dad wasn't homophobic—he was just a little ignorant of certain things. His face when he learned Daniel would be dancing at Pride… "I don't think he'll be there to cheer you on next weekend," I commented dryly.

"As long as you are, I don't care. Today was a good start, don't you think?"

I did. "I see you coped with the lesson about all things football."

He chuckled. "It might have helped when I told him my cousin plays for Arsenal."

I came to a dead stop in the middle of the pavement. "Seriously?"

Daniel laughed. "Did I not mention that?"

"No, you didn't."

He took my hand in his. "That's okay. We have all the time in the world to find out everything about each other."

I didn't care that we were in the middle of my old neighbourhood. I didn't give a toss that curtains were probably twitching up and down the street, and former neighbours were tutting loudly. I shut them out and kissed my boyfriend on the lips.

Daniel cared, however. "Love you." His eyes glistened briefly before he wiped them with his hand.

"Love you too." We relinquished hands and resumed our walk to the station. "I told Mum that, you know," I added.

"What—that you love me?"

I nodded.

"How did she react?"

"She went quiet on me. Said I'd never told her I loved anyone before, not even Cheryl."

"I'm still glowing inside from the fact that you told *her*." He sighed. "I don't want today to end."

He'd taken the words right out of my mouth. "Then it's not going to—at least, not yet." I didn't want to go home. That implied the end to my wonderful weekend, and the start of another week without him while he rehearsed. Plus, there was Pride the following Saturday, and I wouldn't have him to myself until Sunday.

My minutes with Daniel were precious, and I wanted as many of them as possible.

"Can I come home with you?"

Daniel's face lit up. "Of course you can. And you can stay until the last train if you want. I know you'll have to go home eventually, but…"

That gave me another seven or so hours with him, and I knew exactly how we'd be spending them.

Chapter 22

I was still elated by the visit to my parents by the time we reached Daniel's flat. I knew it was early days, but I also knew they'd love Daniel once they got to really know him.

Of course, they'd never love him as much as *I* loved him.

"Do you want a glass of wine?" Daniel called out as he went into the kitchen.

"Yes, please." I walked over to the cream desk below the window, peering at the small wooden book stand on top of it.

They say you can learn a lot about a man by looking at the books he reads. Well, what I saw was illuminating. There was more to my Daniel than met the eye.

My Daniel. Just *thinking* it made me feel good.

"What are you looking at?"

"Your books." I smiled. "The titles make for interesting reading." I read along the spines. "*Making Gay History: The Half-Century Fight for Lesbian and Gay Equal Rights*. *When We Rise*. *The Right Side of History: 100 Years of LGBTQ*

Activism." I glanced at him. "You're not just a pretty face, are you?"

He flushed. "I'm not one for lying down and letting someone trample all over rights that people fought bloody hard for."

I kissed his cheek. "Have I told you recently that I love you?"

"Yes, but you can tell me again."

I cupped his cheek and leaned in until our lips were almost touching. "I love you," I whispered before kissing him, a slow, sensual kiss that I hoped told him about the path I wanted our evening to take. Then I released him and went back to studying his books. It was a fascinating insight, especially when I caught sight of a thin book at the end. I pulled it from its place and stared at the cover. "Oh really?"

"Uh-oh. What have you seen?"

I turned to face him, holding up the book. "*69 Positions of joyful gay sex*?"

Daniel handed me a glass of wine. "Actually, it's funny you should pick that one up. I've been meaning to show it to you."

I put down my glass on the desk and opened the book. Okay, my eyes might have popped out of my head. "And I can see why. There are naked men in here. Getting up to…" I turned the book on its side and stared at one of the photos. "All sorts of things." I smirked. "Does this count as a visual aid?"

Daniel regarded me thoughtfully. "Remember the first time we made love?"

I closed the book and gazed at him. "As if I could forget."

"Well, you said something that stuck with me. You were unhappy that we'd only managed one position. And then you said something about being sure there were more positions than just doggy." He pointed to the book. "I was going to show you this. To let you see there are a *lot* of positions."

I opened the book again. "So I see." I stared at the two models who were demonstrating the positions. "Whoa. He's a… big boy."

Daniel bit his lip. "One, *he* is a porn star by the name of Kriss Evans. And two… I'm only just realizing my boyfriend is a size queen." His eyes twinkled with obvious amusement.

I took a step toward him and reached down to cup his crotch. "And if I am? I lay the blame right… here," I said, giving his dick a gentle squeeze. Then I went back to the book. "Oh my God. They're fucking on the kitchen table." I gaped at the next photo. "On a chair? Are they kidding?" Judging by the precarious position the blond model was in, they were an accident waiting to happen.

And imagine having to explain what happened to the paramedics…

Daniel chuckled. "There are a few where

they use chairs, in a variety of ways. Now, if you want adventure, take a look at number 27."

I narrowed my gaze. "Just how many times have you read this book?"

"Oh, a few," he said lightly.

I flicked through the pages until I found it. "Oh My Fucking God. What are they, acrobats?" Kriss was standing behind the other model, who had all his weight on his forearms. The rest of his body was in the air, his legs wide with Kriss standing between them. I peered at the text. "The *wheelbarrow*?"

Daniel burst out laughing. "Before you ask, I've never tried it." He gently took the book from me. "*This* is the theory. Putting them into practice is something else entirely." He made as if to replace the book on its stand, but I snatched it from him.

"Oh no you don't." When he stared at me, I clutched it against my chest. "You can't say things like that and just leave it. Now we *have* to try some of these out."

Daniel blinked. "You're serious?"

"You're talking to someone who could be called Missionary Man. And I think I've been missing out." I tapped the book with my index finger. "Don't you think some of these could be fun? Although, I'm not sure I could do half of them." I glared at him. "We've already had words about you and your… flexibility."

"Oh, I don't know," Daniel said with a grin. "You managed to get your knees to your ears when I was rimming you." He held out his hand for the book, and I handed it over with a show of reluctance. Daniel flicked through it. "I suppose we *could* see how many of these we can get done before we come."

I squinted at him. "Are we trying to get into the Guinness Book of World Records? Because I'm going to draw the line at having an observer in here to verify it all."

Daniel laughed. "I think there are too many in here to deal with, so let's go with a cut down version." He placed the book on the stand, then got out his phone and scrolled through his pictures. "There. That's a much easier goal to aim for." He held out his phone.

I peered at the image. It was a set of ten positions, drawn with models. I gaped at #8. "No fucking way. We are *not* fucking standing up." One of the models had his arms around his partner's neck, with his legs hooked over the guy's arms—and no other visible means of support. "'Suspended Congress', eh? Er, no. One or both of us could break our necks doing that." I peered at #10. "'Bumper cars'? Who comes up with these names?"

Daniel's eyes gleamed. "Now *that* one looks like fun. And seeing as *you* wanted to try them out, *I'll* be on the receiving end—in the interests of research, of course," he added in a serious tone.

"Oh, of course," I replied, equally serious.

"If only to prove to you that there's more to life than missionary."

I had an idea this was going to be a *lot* of fun.

#LoveWins
love is love

Daniel lay face-down on the coffee table that was covered in pillows with a towel over them all. My weight was on my hands as I rocked into his tight arse, both of us with our feet off the floor.

Daniel moaned as I filled him, taking it slow. "Hey… don't get too comfortable in this position. We're not done… having fun yet."

I grinned. "Says who? Maybe I've had enough fun." I pulled virtually the whole way out of him, only to drive deep at the last minute. "See?" I said as he groaned again. "This is fun."

"So was Pirate's Bounty," he gasped out.

I paused, letting him take my weight, my dick buried in his hole. "Oh yeah. You had fun with that one. 'Put your leg up here. No, higher. Higher!'

He chuckled. "I bet you never realized your

leg could move like that. But you enjoyed Cowboy and Reverse Cowboy, didn't you?" Another chuckle. "Judging by the cries of 'Giddy-up, gee-gee!' that you kept shouting out."

I kissed his shoulders, rolling my hips just a little. "And you had to be the bucking bronco, didn't you? Because at one point it felt like you were trying to throw me off."

Daniel turned his head slightly, grinning. "But it was fun. Not as much fun as the Arch, though."

I leaned in, my lips brushing his ear. "Which we are never doing, ever again." I almost put my back out, while Daniel—Mr Lithe and Supple, 2018—looked like he was doing a great crab, that stand from gymnastics that we all tried doing as little kids? "You were just showing off."

"Just one more?"

As if I could say no to that face. "Okay. One more."

"Put your hands to the floor at the side of the table. You're going to turn yourself around until you're facing the other way… but keep your dick inside me."

"Are you for real?" I panted.

"You can do it!"

I put one hand down to the floor, holding onto the edge of the coffee table with the other, and carefully and slowly tried to spin myself around in a half-circle, doing my best not to dislodge my cock.

Except Daniel was spinning with me.

"I thought you were supposed to stay still?" I blurted out.

"I'm trying! But you keep dragging me with you."

"Then hold onto the table or something."

Then I got the giggles, and they proved infectious. The pair of us were laughing like hyenas. "Okay," I said when I got myself under control. "Let's try that again." This time I managed it and put my hands to the ground between his legs. "Now what?"

"Now rock like you were doing before." Daniel tilted his hips, and I drove my dick into him, rocking back and forth on my hands. "That's it, baby. We did it! Bumper Cars!"

I was too busy enjoying the delicious friction of my dick in his arse.

"Are you getting close?" he asked.

"Yeah." His body tight around my shaft felt amazing. "We're done now, right? I can come now, yeah?"

Daniel laughed. "You've worked through Doggy, Cowboy, Reverse Cowboy, Pirate's Bounty, Spooning, the Arch, and now Bumper Cars. I think seven positions is varied enough for one night, don't you? Because I *know* my arse will still be feeling the aftereffects in the morning. So yeah, it's time to come."

Thank God for that. We were both covered in sweat, and we'd laughed a lot. Now all I wanted to do was come. "Do we get to do one of them again for a finish? Because I don't think I've got the energy to fuck you standing up. Plus, I think I'd drop you."

"You're off the hook. Now it's *my* turn," Daniel announced. "Put the towel on the sofa and lie on it, on your back."

I was intrigued. I pulled free of him and arranged the sofa as he'd instructed. Daniel grabbed one of the pillows and stuffed it under my arse, raising me up a little. Then I moaned as Daniel knelt beside the sofa and slid a lube-slick finger inside me.

"Got to get you ready for me," he said, his voice a little husky. By the time he had two fingers sliding in and out, I was more than ready. Daniel lubed up his bare cock, climbed onto the sofa, and lifted my legs into the air.

I blinked, grabbing them. "We're doing… missionary?" I admit, that wasn't what I'd envisioned for a grand finale.

Daniel knelt at my arse and guided his dick into position. "The great thing about missionary," he said as he slowly filled me, "is that with your legs like this, it makes your hole nice and tight."

Fuck, he wasn't kidding.

"And I get to go deep," he added, his cock all the way inside me.

I shuddered.

Daniel leaned in, his full weight behind his cock, and fuck, I was full. He placed his hands flat to the seat cushion and bent over to kiss me. "But the best thing?" He rolled his hips, and fireworks went off inside me. "I get to hit your prostate. Every single time if I want." He looked into my eyes. "And I want."

I had time to catch my breath before he began, driving his dick into me with short, quick thrusts that felt like nothing he'd done before. I cupped his nape and dragged him down into a kiss as he pistoned in and out of my arse, and all I could do was hold on. The only words to leave my lips during this erotic onslaught were "Oh fuck," "Oh yeah," and a whole lot of *oh*s as he nailed my prostate with impressive accuracy. I grabbed his arse cheeks, his thighs, I smacked his thighs as if spurring him on…

Daniel lifted my legs higher until my ankles rested against his shoulders, then he thrust hard, and a loud cry burst from me.

"You like that," he stated, his hips rolling.

"Love it," I sobbed, my whole body shaking. I clung to him, my fingers digging into his back, his arse cheeks, his thighs.

"You love my cock in your arse?"

"Yes!" Fuck, I was losing it. It was as if he'd flicked a switch and my body was on fire, every cell and fibre alight. Without a touch, my dick pulsed come onto my chest, but he didn't stop.

"That's one. You've got at least another load in you."

"Daniel!"

He slowed down, rotating his dick inside me, and oh my *God*, that felt incredible. "Take a breath," he said with a smile. "Because I'm just getting warmed up for the final page."

God help me, I wasn't going to make it. "Has anyone ever died from being fucked?" Because there was no other word for what we were doing.

"I think you're safe," he said, moving sinuously, sliding deep and slow into me. "Break over. Any last requests?"

"Fuck me," I begged.

"With pleasure." Then he drove hard into me, and I knew I didn't have long. I locked my legs around his waist and held onto him as he rocked into me again and again, those same cries falling from my lips as Daniel brought me to the edge. My hands were everywhere: on his head, his nape, his back, his arse, his thighs… I couldn't keep still, and I clutched the towel beneath my hips, holding onto it as if it would keep me from tumbling over the edge.

Then Daniel filled me to the hilt, and I fell.

Heat covered my belly as I shot again, although nowhere near as hard as the first time, and I moaned from the sheer pleasure that burst through me. Daniel bowed his head and buried his face in my neck, and I groaned at the feel of yet more heat, only this time it was inside me.

"I love you," he whispered, his weight on me as he shuddered through his orgasm, I locked my arms around his neck and kissed him, unwilling to let go of him for a second. We exchanged breathless kisses and soft murmurs, none of it making much sense, but I didn't care.

When I could breathe normally, I looked him in the eye. "I will *never* complain about missionary ever again."

A second later, Daniel burst out laughing and I joined him, the laughter ejecting his spent dick from my body. I grinned. "Okay. Get Guinness on the phone."

Daniel brushed my damp hair away from my forehead. "Can we get cleaned up before they turn up with cameras?"

I wrinkled my nose. "I think a shower is definitely in order." I groaned as I straightened my legs. "I need to get fitter if our sex life is going to be this vigorous."

Daniel chuckled. "Trust me. It gets easier with practice."

I sighed happily, before kissing him on the lips. "I see a lot of practice in my future."

Hey, if they ever announce that sex is going to be an Olympic event, I want to be ready, okay?

Because Daniel and I would be aiming for

gold.

#LoveWins

love is love

Pride, July 7, 2018

As soon as my phone rang, I knew it was Daniel. “Hi. You all done?”

“Yeah. We just got off the stage. But I can’t see you in the crowd. Where are you?”

“The Boathouse Cafe, Regent’s Park.”

Silence for a moment. “What on earth are you doing there?”

I chuckled. “Waiting for you?”

“Give me half an hour. I’d normally walk it, no problem, but I’m knackered.”

“I’ll have a cold drink waiting for you. And maybe an ice cream.”

“You angel! I love you. See you soon.” He disconnected.

I sat on my bench and gazed out at the lake. Lots of little kids were feeding the ducks who were quacking and squabbling with much flapping of wings to get to the bread. I waited about twenty-five minutes before I went to the cafe and bought two icy cans of Coke. Then I returned to my bench.

Within two minutes of that, Daniel arrived. He’d changed into his jeans, but his makeup was still in evidence, as was the rainbow feather boa around his neck. A rainbow bag was slung over his shoulder. He looked tired but happy.

I stood to kiss him and got an exuberant kiss in return. Then he dropped onto the bench beside me, grabbed the can I'd placed there, and held it against the back of his neck.

"God, that feels good." He peered at me. "Did you see the parade?"

"I saw *you*, briefly. You were amazing, but then I had no doubt you would be." I peered at his feet and smirked. "I see you changed out of your heels."

"Excuse me? Using all the stairs at the station, in heels? I'd break my neck." He frowned. "You said briefly. That implies you didn't stay. Why not?"

How the hell could I tell him without sounding like a complete wuss?

Then it struck me. I didn't want there to be secrets between us.

"I think it was a case of sensory overload. Too many people, too much noise, too hot…"

He nodded. "I've never known it be so hot for Pride."

"And then there was all that mess at the start."

Daniel widened his eyes. "Did you see the protesters?"

"The anti-trans brigade, lying down in front

of the parade? Oh yeah, I saw them. I was amazed they were allowed to walk, to be honest."

"*I* was amazed no one got hurt. They shouldn't have been allowed to lead the march." He gave me a compassionate glance. "So… not a good first Pride for you then."

"I had no idea there'd be that many people," I confessed. "If I'd been with someone, it might have been better. As it was, I just got swallowed up by the crowds."

"Didn't you see Mick and Pete? I thought they were going too."

I chuckled. "I think they saw less of the march than I did, before Pete dragged Mick to his hotel. Mick texted me about an hour ago. Told me not to expect him home tonight."

Daniel's eyes gleamed. "Sounds like they had a good Pride though." He opened his can. "I'd better drink this before my body heat warms it to the temperature of tea." He took a long swallow, and I tried not to stare at his Adam's apple bobbing in his long, graceful neck.

"Better?"

"Much." Daniel leaned against the bench. "Don't worry. There's always next year."

"I'll do better next year," I assured him. I was determined to be there and cheer him on for the entire parade.

"Now, hadn't you better text Justin or Niall?"

I gave him a perplexed glance. "Do I need to text them?"

Daniel grinned. "Yes, you do. They need to know you're not coming home tonight either."

"Oh?" Now I was grinning too. "And where will I be?"

He leaned in until his mouth was inches from mine. "At my place. In my bed. Naked, with every bloody window in the place open. Eating pizza and watching DVDs."

"And what are we watching?"

His eyes sparkled. "I have a box set of Dante's Cove. Think gay men and dark, mystical forces. Sort of a cross between Buffy the Vampire Slayer and Queer as Folk."

"Is it good?"

Daniel coughed. "No, but we're not exactly watching it for the plot."

I frowned. "Oh. Then why are we—*Oh*." This sounded promising.

He grinned. "*Now* he gets it. And we might need to take several showers during the evening."

I nodded. "Because of the heat."

Daniel's lips twitched. "Oh. Yeah. That too."

I gave him a suspicious glance. "I thought you were knackered."

"What can I say? You work miracles. One look at you and I've found my second wind." Daniel got to his feet and held out his hand to me.

"Come on, let's go. I need to strip off and get wet." He grinned. "I'll let you wash my back. And anywhere else you take a fancy to."

Well, how could a boy say no to an offer like that?

Epilogue

Pride, July 6, 2019

I hurried through the crowded streets, aware of the time. I hadn't intended staying so long in the LGBTQ helpline tent in Soho Square, but when that young guy turned up, looking like he desperately needed to talk, I knew I had to see if I could help.

As it turned out, I was the one he'd opened up to, and we sat in the corner of the tent, drinking water, me doing the listening while he did most of the talking. He was seventeen, shy, and confused as hell because he liked girls *and* boys. We chatted for what seemed like ages, and when he finally left, he was smiling, clutching a wad of leaflets, and with cards for him to call if he needed help.

And I was left feeling energized. I'd helped someone.

It was only then I realized I was missing the parade. More importantly, I was missing watching my boyfriend dance. I said goodbye to the people doing their stint in the tent, and hurried through the streets of Soho, heading for Piccadilly Circus. That was no easy task: by now the number of people out to see the parade had increased, and navigating through the crowds grew more difficult the closer I got to the parade. As I drew nearer to Eros where I was meeting Rachel and Ben, the crowds grew denser still, and for the last few hundred feet I was inching my way through throngs of people decked out in rainbow colours. The mood was fantastic. The parade made its way along the road, flanked by police officers, most of whom had the obligatory rainbow stripe painted on their cheek, and some of whom were on the receiving end of kisses from the general public, not to mention some of the performers. The officers appeared to take it all in their stride, grinning and posing for selfies.

Gotta love the British police force. When they get it right, they *really* get it right.

I reached Eros and scanned the assembled throng, looking for Rachel. It felt like there were even more people gathered than the previous year, holding up huge banners and waving flags of all colours. What I noticed most?

All the colours of the LGBTQA spectrum were on display.

"Lee!"

I followed the sound of her voice and found them standing on the edge of the pavement. Ben wore a sling across his front, in which was my little six-month-old niece, Amber. Rachel gave me a beaming smile, and stroked Amber's head. "Hey, Amber, look. It's Buncle Lee."

I gave Rachel a mock glare, before hugging her and greeting Ben. I gave my niece a kiss on the head. "Sorry I'm late."

"We were beginning to think you weren't coming," Rachel teased.

"As if I'd miss Amber's first Pride," I joked.

"I'm pretty sure Amber won't remember a thing about it," Ben said with a chuckle. He glanced at the strap of my bag slung across my chest and tapped one of my pins. "Nice."

It was my Bi Pride pin. Daniel had got it for me. I beamed. "As some wise person once said, I'm the B in LGBTQA."

Rachel laughed. "Gee, I wonder who that was."

"Your second Pride," Ben remarked. "Is it much different from the first?"

I laughed. "At least I got to see more of it this year." *I* was certainly different. A lot had happened in the year since then, the most important event being me moving into Daniel's flat just before Amber was born. (Well, he couldn't very well move into my *room*, now could he?) I was sad to say goodbye to the guys, but we'd stayed in touch. I wasn't the only one to move out—Pete had made the move from Edinburgh, and he and Mick had bought a house in Surrey. Daniel and I often went there for a weekend, and the four of us had become great friends.

"And in answer to your question, yes and no," I replied with a smile. I looked around. "Where's Gary? Is he not coming this year?"

Ben chuckled. "Oh, he's here, all right. He's with his new boyfriend. They've gone to Freedom."

"So that's the last we'll see of *him* until tonight," Rachel concluded.

"About time you got here," came a voice from behind me. I whirled around to greet Caroline with a hug. She looked amazing in a rainbow dress that clung to her petite frame. "Daniel said I might see you here." She nodded hello to Rachel and Ben, then addressed me. "Troy says hi. He's working on the main stage, so you'll see him later."

I peered at the parade. "Have you seen Daniel yet?" I couldn't hear the music from their float, but I knew they were due to stop and perform at the statue.

"Enough times that I've now heard all twelve songs at least twice," she said with a grin. "They should be along any minute. How was the booth?"

"It was good," I admitted. It had been Caroline's idea to help out, and I'd jumped at the chance. Daniel was doing his bit, so the least I could do was volunteer to man the booth and talk to anyone who wanted advice.

"Would you do it again, there's the question?"

I grinned. "In a heartbeat."

"Are you and Daniel coming to lunch at Molly and Geoff's tomorrow?" Ben asked.

"As if we'd miss Sunday lunch with the family." Mum had said she was doing a roast turkey for a change, and she wanted Daniel to make his parmesan baked parsnips to go with it. Daniel was trying to improve his culinary repertoire. He'd made the dish at Christmas, and Mum had been blown away. And Dad wanted Daniel's advice on which barbecue to buy, now that he'd decided to switch to a gas powered one.

Another change since the last Pride was that Daniel had taken me to meet Ella and Rick, his foster parents. They were a sweet couple, and just looking at the wall full of photos of all the LGBT kids they'd fostered over the years, told me how special they were.

"Here they come!" Rachel shouted. She tugged me to stand in front of her, so I got a great view of the dance troupe's float. All the men wore purple tank tops with a rainbow across their chests, and tight purple shorts that left nothing to the imagination. I could still recall my reaction when Daniel modelled the costume for the first time.

Yeah. Neither of us got a lot of sleep that night.

Daniel was one of ten dancers walking behind the float, and he waved enthusiastically as soon as he saw me.

"Oh my God, how does he walk in those heels?" Ben exclaimed.

"With a lot of patience and practice," I responded. Daniel had been wearing them every night around the flat for most of June. I definitely hadn't complained, especially that one evening when the heels were all he wore.

What can I say? He keeps finding buttons I never knew I had, and then he makes sure he presses them. Which makes *me* a very happy boy.

The float came to a dead stop, and music blared out from the huge speakers set up at the back of it.

I had to smile. It was Bruno Mars' Marry You.

"Oh, here we go again," Caroline said with a smile. "This is their third time with this number, so they should have all their moves perfected by now."

"I'll have you know they had all their moves perfected long before today." Daniel and the troupe had put in a great many hours this year.

The dancers started pulling spectators into the road.

"What are they doing?"

"Oh, they each grab an onlooker and dance with them. It's really cute," Caroline told me. "Especially when they get down on one knee and pretend to propose to them."

When Daniel advanced on me, his eyes sparkling, I wagged my finger. "Oh no you don't."

"Aw, come on, baby. Dance with me." He pouted, his lips glistening with pink gloss. His sparkly purple eye shadow looked amazing. "If I can't dance with you at *Pride*…"

I never could refuse him. And it *was* Pride, right?

I allowed him to lead me into the road, and suddenly the dancers synchronized their movements, while the spectators stood in front of each dancer, laughing and looking awkward while the men danced around them.

I was no different. I wasn't about to try and dance—that was Daniel's job.

The atmosphere was brilliant, with the people thronged on either side of the road videoing the routine. Rachel yelled at me to look at her, and I saw she had her phone out too, as did Caroline. I waved for the cameras as Daniel danced around me and in front of me, and as always, I admired the way his body moved to the music.

The routine was almost at an end, when suddenly the dancers flocked to Daniel, gathering around him in a semicircle. I had no idea he was leading this number. When the line demanding the girl to just say *I do* came over the speakers, Daniel got down on one knee—and pulled a small black velvet box from the pocket of his shorts.

Oh fuck.

My heartbeat matched the bass rhythm thudding out from the speakers. All around me, the spectators caught wind of what was going on, and were cheering and applauding. So many phones appeared as onlookers took pictures and video.

It was obvious from the dancers around Daniel that they were all in on it.

"Go on then. Ask him," one of them shouted. The crowd picked it up, and suddenly everyone was chanting "Ask him! Ask him!"

Daniel gazed around him and laughed. "Give me a chance then!" His eyes were focused on me as he opened the box, revealing the plain gold band. And when he mouthed the lyrics, I thought I was going to die of happiness right there in the middle of the road.

The song ended, and he looked me in the eye. "Well? *Am* I gonna marry you?"

I nodded. "Yes," I whispered.

The dancers around him grinned. "We can't hear you, Lee," one of them shouted, cupping his ear as the others laughed.

"Yes, I'll marry you," I yelled at the top of my voice. The applause and cheers from the crowd erupted, drowning out everything else.

Daniel's face lit up, and he was up off his knee and taking me in his arms in a flash. He kissed me as if his life depended on it, and I gave as good as I got. His fellow dancers thronged around us, patting him on the back and hugging both of us. In all of the noise and excitement, Daniel somehow got the ring onto my finger.

I love you, he mouthed.

Love you too, I mouthed back at him. My heart was still dancing up there somewhere in the blue cloudless sky.

Daniel glanced over at Rachel. "Thanks for getting him here," he shouted above the applause and cheers that still rang out.

"You're welcome—brother-in-law-to-be," she replied with a grin. "Anything to help."

I gaped at her. "You… you *knew*?"

I had the sneakiest sister in the world. Which made Daniel the sneakiest fiancé.

Oh my God. I have a fiancé.

The music changed, and Daniel released me. "We've got to go," he said, his face falling. "But I don't want to."

"I know. Me neither." I didn't want this moment to end, but the parade was far from over. "I'll meet you in Trafalgar Square, okay?" Then I grabbed his face and kissed him again. "Love you."

"Love you too, babe." He caressed my cheek. "You said yes." He sounded as though he still didn't believe it.

"Of course I did."

"Daniel, put him down. We've gotta go!" That was Mac, tapping on his watch.

Reluctantly Daniel let go of me, then glanced over my shoulder at Rachel, Ben, and

Caroline. "Look after my fiancé for me till I'm done?"

I didn't think I was ever going to tire of hearing that word. There was only one word that could improve on it—husband.

"We will. We'll make sure he doesn't stumble into traffic in his dazed state," Ben said with a grin.

I was about to dispute that with him when I realized Ben had nailed it.

I was dazed and excited and stupid in love.

Daniel let go of my hand, and the parade moved on. I stood there, gazing at the ring glinting on my left hand.

Rachel put her arm around me. "Let's go somewhere a bit quieter and have a drink. What do you say?"

Before I could reply, Caroline chipped in. "Somewhere with a porn star martini."

I grinned. "*Now* you're talking." The four of us—five including little Amber—weaved our way through the crowd, away from the noise and music and horns blaring. A drink sounded perfect.

I'd wait for Daniel, and then we'd go home on the train, together.

Just the two of us.

The End

#loveWins
love is love

About the author

K.C. Wells lives on an island off the south coast of the UK, surrounded by natural beauty. She writes about men who love men, and can't even contemplate a life that doesn't include writing.
The rainbow rose tattoo on her back with the words 'Love is Love' and 'Love Wins' is her way of hoisting a flag. She plans to be writing about men in love - be it sweet and slow, hot or kinky - for a long while to come.

Available titles

<u>Learning to Love</u>
Michael & Sean
Evan & Daniel
Josh & Chris
Final Exam

<u>Sensual Bonds</u>
A Bond of Three
A Bond of Truth

<u>Merrychurch Mysteries</u>
Truth Will Out
Roots of Evil
A Novel Murder (Coming August 2020)

<u>Love, Unexpected</u>
Debt
Burden

<u>Dreamspun Desires</u>
The Senator's Secret
Out of the Shadows
My Fair Brady
Under the Covers

Love Lessons Learned
First
Waiting for You
Step by Step

Bromantically Yours
BFF

<ins>Collars & Cuffs</ins>
An Unlocked Heart
Trusting Thomas
Someone to Keep Me (K.C. Wells & Parker Williams)
A Dance with Domination
Damian's Discipline (K.C. Wells & Parker Williams)
Make Me Soar
Dom of Ages (K.C. Wells & Parker Williams)
Endings and Beginnings (K.C. Wells & Parker Williams)

<ins>Secrets – with Parker Williams</ins>
Before You Break
An Unlocked Mind
Threepeat
On the Same Page

<ins>Personal</ins>
Making it Personal
Personal Changes
More than Personal
Personal Secrets
Strictly Personal
Personal Challenges
Confetti, Cake & Confessions
Confetti, Coriandoli e Confessioni

Connections
Saving Jason
A Christmas Promise
The Law of Miracles

Anthologies

Fifty Gays of Shade
Winning Will's Heart

Come, Play
Watch and Learn

Writing as Tantalus
Damon & Pete: Playing with Fire

Auf deutsch

Schuld

Dreamspun Desires
Der Verlobte des Senators
Als die Einsamkeit wich

Zum Ersten Mal Liebe
Schritt für Schritt
Gestern, Jetzt und Auf Ewig

Collars & Cuffs
Herz Ohne Fesseln
Vertrauen in Thomas

Persönlich
Persönliche Entscheidungen
Persönliche Veränderungen
Mehr als Persönliche
Persönliche Geheimnisse
Streng Persönlich

En français

In italiano

Una Questione Personale
Cambiamenti Personali
Piú che personale
Segreti Personali
Strettamente personale
Sfide personali

Confetti, Coriandoli e Confessioni

Per Salvare Jason

<u>Island Tales</u>
Le Maree di Settembre
In Attesa di un Principe
Piegarsi alle tenebre

<u>Lightning Tales</u>
Il Professore
Fidati di me

<u>A Material World</u>
Pizzo
Satin
Seta
Denim

Scambio di ruoli

<u>Writing as Tantalus</u>
Damon & Pete: Giocare col fuoco

Made in the USA
Monee, IL
19 January 2021

58051064R00184